Finding Hope

A Chance and a Hope

Book Two

SJ McCoy

A Sweet n Steamy Romance

Published by Xenion, Inc

Finding Hope Copyright © SJ McCoy 2017

Published by Xenion, Inc.
First Paperback edition 2017
www.sjmccoy.com

Cover Design by Dana Lamothe of Designs by Dana
Editor: Mitzi Pummer Carroll
Proofreader: Aileen Blomberg and Marisa Nichols

ISBN 978-1-946220-25-7

Pretty Please, Read This First!

I'm going for a change of tactic this time. I hope the pretty please has you here reading this and that you haven't gone straight to Chapter Twenty-One wondering how I got my numbering so mixed up. Books don't normally start with Chapter Twenty-One before going to Chapter One, but then I'm not very good at doing normal.

There is method in my madness. I wanted to start this story by including the last chapter of Chance Encounter. You may have read it, you may not. That depends on whether you wanted to read the cliffhanger. If you didn't, you can now learn what happened before Chance and Hope left Oregon. Even if you did read it and have been cursing me for the last month ;0) you might want to read it again before you dive into Finding Hope. I hope you'll enjoy this second part of Chance and Hope's story. I love them both. The third and final book, Give Hope a Chance will be coming out July 11.

Anyway, that's enough from me. I'll get out of the way and let you read it.

Love

SJ

oxo

Chapter Twenty One

Chance woke with a start. He looked around, wondering what he'd heard. Nothing, it seemed. He lay there for a few moments thinking about tomorrow. This was the last night he'd lie beside her, at least for now. He still didn't know when he'd see her again. Part of him still wasn't sure that he should see her again. It seemed to him he'd caused her enough trouble already. And when it came to him, much as he wanted to see where things could go, part of him just wanted to go back to his life, back to his comfort zone. Hope was amazing. He cared about her, but maybe his dad had raised a coward. Maybe it would be better, easier for them both, if they stuck with their original plan and just said goodbye tomorrow—if they saved each other as a beautiful memory and didn't try for more. He sighed. He wanted more, though. He'd gone to visit Chloe's grave before he came out here to tell her that he was ready to start living again. Now he'd met a woman he might want to share his life with. If he ran away from the possibility now, he doubted he'd ever try again.

He rolled over onto his side, but he couldn't get comfortable. He got up and headed downstairs for a drink of water. Staring out the patio doors at the moonlight dancing on the ocean, he started to feel as though all this had just been a dream. Tomorrow, he'd wake up and go back to his real life. All this would be over, unless he really wanted to work to make it happen between them. He started at the sound of a bleep and turned around to see Hope's phone light up. She'd left it on the countertop to charge. It bleeped again. He felt guilty as he stepped toward it, wondering who was messaging her in the middle of the night. He checked the clock—two thirty-five in the morning, to be precise. The screen lit up again and he stared down at the notifications.

> *Hope call me. Did he tell you he has a criminal record?*
> *I want you away from that man.*
>
> *Please Hope. I'm concerned about you.*
> *Make sure goodbye means goodbye tomorrow.*
> *I don't want you around him.*
> *Call me in the morning.*

Chance closed his eyes and sighed. He nodded slowly. What father wouldn't feel that way? He couldn't blame the guy. He was looking out for his daughter. He didn't know the whole story. Chance was glad that Hope did. It hadn't been easy to share his past with her, but having her hear it from someone else would have been worse.

What was he supposed to do? He couldn't exactly call the guy and explain himself. Even if he did, he doubted it'd make any difference. Men like that weren't forgiving about mistakes, especially criminal ones.

Another text came in.

> *Please Hope. We've come so far in the last few years. Don't throw it away over some no-good ranch hand.*

That was like a dagger to Chance's heart. Not being called a no-good ranch hand, he could handle that. No, the thought that Hope and her dad had been getting closer, and that he was about to screw things up between them. He couldn't handle that. He knew what it was like to be estranged from your father. He knew how good it felt to finally be close again. He rested his head in his hands. He knew what he had to do. There was no way he would come between Hope and her dad. No matter what future might have been possible between the two of them, he'd give it all up right here and now in order to protect her relationship with her dad.

He tiptoed back upstairs and picked his clothes up, glad that he had everything packed and ready to go. He looked down at her, wanting so badly to reach out and touch her, but not daring to in case he woke her.

He kissed his fingertips and blew the kiss to her, hoping that somehow she'd feel it and know that he cared.

He went back downstairs and got dressed then gathered his things together. He went back to the kitchen and picked up the notepad he'd written his number on for her that first day they met. It was only two weeks ago, but it felt like so much longer.

He picked up the pen and stared at the paper. What could he tell her? What could he say? He couldn't tell her why he was leaving. If he tried to tell how he felt about her he'd still be here writing by the time she woke up. He stared at the paper a long time before he finally got it. He had to make himself out to be an asshole. That way she'd hate him; she wouldn't want to come after him, and she wouldn't upset her dad. Her dad could step in as her hero to pick up the pieces – and be proved right.

He scribbled a few words and picked up his bag. For one crazy moment, he wanted to put it down again, get undressed and go back and hold her in his arms. They could face all of this tomorrow. Together. But no. Together wasn't a way he got to live life. He was supposed to be alone; he should never have forgotten that. Hope was someone who deserved to be happy, and she would no doubt be happier without him.

With a sad smile, he made sure he locked the front door as he let himself out and closed it gently behind him. He threw his bag in the car and drove away without once looking back.

~ ~ ~

Hope opened her eyes and stretched, then turned over to look at Chance. This was the last time they'd get to wake up together until she could get up to Montana to visit him. Her smile faded when her gaze landed on an empty pillow. She was sad that he'd gotten up and left her, robbing them of this one last time. She sat up and shook her head. Perhaps she was being a little bit melodramatic there. It wasn't such a big deal. She got out of bed and pulled her robe on. He wasn't in the bathroom. He must be downstairs already.

By the time she reached the kitchen, she knew he wasn't there. The house was empty; she knew it. Maybe he'd gone for a walk on the beach? But would he really do that without waking her to go with him? She didn't think so.

She went to pick up her phone. She needed to call him; she had a horrible feeling in the pit of her stomach. Something was wrong. Very wrong. As she reached for her phone, she saw the note. Tears pricked her eyes as she read it. She picked it up and read it again. It was so short, no explanation; no, nothing but a few words. No! He wouldn't do that.

But apparently, he had.

Sorry, honey, but this is where the cowboy rides away.

She put the note back down on the table and let the tears begin to fall;

Chapter One

Chance tried to ignore the banging on the door. He rolled onto his side and pulled the covers up over his head. That didn't work; the banging continued, growing louder. He burrowed his head under his pillow and covered it with his arms.

"Open up, Chance. I know you're in there." It was Mason.

Chance groaned. "Go away."

"No such luck. I'm coming in."

"Leave me in peace. It's my day off." He heard the front door creak as it opened. For the first time, he wished this was a place where he felt the need to lock his door. He listened to Mason's boots cross the living room and approach the bedroom. "I'm pretty sure I told you to go away."

"Tough. I'm going nowhere."

Chance blew out a big sigh and threw the pillow in the direction of Mason's voice.

Mason laughed. "Wow. Getting a pillow thrown at me is a whole lot easier to handle than what I thought I might get."

"What you still will get if you don't fuck off within the next thirty seconds."

Mason laughed again. "There's no need to wait thirty seconds. Like I said, I'm going nowhere, so whatever you're going to do, you may as well get on with it."

Chance reluctantly rolled over and sat up. "And I thought I was a stubborn bastard."

Mason smiled. "You sure as hell are, but I'm right there with you. Just ask Gina."

Chance nodded and rubbed his hand over his face. His stubble felt more like beard now, but it hardly mattered.

Mason watched him. "Are you planning on shaving anytime soon? You look like shit."

"Thanks. If you want bright-eyed and bushy-tailed, go find yourself a fucking squirrel."

Mason laughed. "Nah. I'll stick around for red-eyed and whiskered, but if there's any chance you could find your way into the shower, I'd appreciate it. I'll even make you some coffee while you're in there."

Chance glowered at him for a moment. He had no right coming in here, no right to tell him he needed a shower, no right to ... He blew out a sigh and nodded. "Okay, but make it strong."

Mason was waiting for him in the kitchen when he was showered and dressed. He thrust a mug of coffee toward him, and Chance took it with a grunt of thanks.

"You got any plans for the day?"

Chance narrowed his eyes at him. "Well, I was thinking about heading over to Bozeman, doing a little shopping at Macy's, getting a manicure, and then having a spot of lunch at the Open Range. How about you?"

Mason rolled his eyes. "There's no need to be sarcastic."

Chance shrugged and took a gulp of his coffee. Man, he needed that. "Well, there's no need for you to be so damned superficial, is there? You don't come in here, drag me out of my pit, and then make polite small talk like we're a couple of chicks planning a girly day out. Just tell me what you really want or fuck off and leave me alone."

Mason's jaw set and his eyebrows came down, in a look that Chance recognized but had never had turned on him before. "What do I want? I want you to stop being an asshole. I want you to accept that I'm worried about you. I want you to come back."

Chance could feel himself shutting down with every word Mason spoke. His eyes narrowed. His lips pressed together. His grip on his coffee mug tightened and his shoulders set with tension.

"Come on. Say something!"

"What? What do you want me to say? Sorry, I can't stop being an asshole. It comes naturally. You're worried about me? That's your choice. It's nothing I have any control over. And come back? What the fuck does that even mean? I've been back a month."

Mason shook his head and sat down heavily across the table from him. The stubbornness was gone from his face. His eyes were full of concern. "Yeah, physically you've been back from Oregon for a month. But you haven't really been here, and we both know it. You've shut down. I get that; you do that. But you've shut me out; you've never done that before. I don't know how to handle it, Chance."

"There's nothing to handle. I'm fine."

Mason shrugged. "Maybe you are, I wouldn't know. But I'm not. I miss my friend."

Chance closed his eyes against the tears that pricked suddenly. He couldn't handle that. He needed to feel angry; he needed to feel hurt. He didn't need to feel he was letting Mason down.

"I'm sorry. I know that's not your problem, and it seems you've got enough problems of your own, but I miss you. I thought after all these years we could turn to each other."

Mason shrugged. "I guess we can't. I guess I'm just talking like a chick again." He drained the last of his coffee. "I'm sorry I ruined your morning. You know where I am if ever you want to talk." He got up and grabbed his hat from the hook on the back of the door.

"Sit back down, asshole. Since you got me out of bed, you may as well stick around."

Mason's lips turned up in the tiniest hint of a smile. "Only if you want me to."

Chance let out a reluctant laugh. "You're going to make me say it?"

Mason chuckled. "Yep."

"Okay. Stay." Mason raised an eyebrow and Chance gave him a rueful smile. "Please."

Mason went and poured himself a fresh coffee and sat back down. "Are you ever going to tell me what happened?"

Chance shook his head. "There's not much point."

"And why's that?"

"Because it's over. Done with. All I can do is put her out of my mind. Forget about it."

Mason raised an eyebrow. "And how's that going?"

Chance shrugged. How could he admit that he couldn't get his mind off Hope no matter what he tried? He couldn't forget her. She was what kept him awake at night.

"But you don't want to talk about it?"

"Like I said, there's no point. Talking about it can't change it."

"But talking about things can make you feel better, even when you can't change them."

Chance sighed. "It's not going to make me feel any better. The best we could hope for is that me talking about it might satisfy your curiosity."

Mason gave him a half smile. "Yeah, there is that."

Chance nodded slowly. Talking about it wasn't going to change the way he felt about Hope, and it wasn't going to change the impossibility of their situation, but maybe Mason was right; maybe talking would make him feel a little better. It couldn't hurt. "So, what do you want to know?"

"Everything! The last time I talked to you in Oregon you weren't sure if you were going to even see Hope again. Then the two of you were splashed all over the headlines, and I thought you'd decided to go all in. But after that no one knew where you were for days until you showed up back here— saying that it had all been a mistake, there was nothing to talk about, and you were over it."

Chance nodded. "That about sums up everything that happened. So, what else is it you want to know?"

Mason frowned at him. "That might be what happened, but I want to know why. I'll admit I was happy for you when I saw the two of you in the papers. Gina even recorded a segment they did on one of the TV gossip shows. You made a striking couple, you know. And unless she's completely changed since she was a kid, she's a real sweetheart."

Chance cocked his head to one side. "You knew her when you were kids?"

"Not exactly knew her, no, but we used to see her out around town every now and then. Her and her cousins."

Chance nodded. "She hasn't changed. She's a good person. She's smart and sweet and straightforward …" His words trailed away as he remembered her smiling at him, remembered so many little things about her.

"So, why aren't the two of you living out the fairy tale happy ending that the press was forecasting for you?"

Chance shrugged. "Didn't anyone ever tell you fairy tales aren't real, and the press is full of shit?"

Mason nodded. "I guess, but I had a feeling, I really thought …" He shrugged. "Are you going to tell me what went wrong?"

"Yeah. It wouldn't have worked." He nodded. He was still trying to convince himself of that. Every day since he'd been back he'd told himself over and over that it wouldn't have worked out, that it was best this way. He looked up and met Mason's gaze. "For a little while there we'd decided that we were going to give it a shot. She was going to come up here to visit me." He looked away again, remembering how that had felt. He shrugged. "But you know who her dad is, right?"

Mason nodded.

"Well, it seems he decided to check out who I am—and he didn't like what he found."

"But …"

Chance held up a hand. "Come on, Mase. You have to understand that, especially now. Think about little Phoenix. If you found out that she was seeing a guy who had the kind of past I do, would you be happy about it?"

"No, but I'd want to see her happy. I'd want to meet the guy. Find out for myself what he was really like. I wouldn't just judge him on his history."

Chance raised an eyebrow. "You say that now, but I think it'd be a different matter if it came down to it."

Mason nodded grudgingly. "Maybe. So, he didn't want her seeing you anymore, and she just obeyed him?"

Chance closed his eyes. "Not exactly."

"Then what, exactly? There's something you're not telling me, isn't there?"

"Yeah. See, the way I found out that her dad wasn't happy about it was …" Chance wasn't sure he even wanted to tell Mason. He'd second-guessed himself so many times over his decision to walk out on her in the middle of the night.

"Was what?" asked Mason impatiently.

"On our last night. I got up for a drink of water. Her phone was bleeping away. Her dad was sending her text after text, telling her he wanted her away from me. That I had a criminal record. That … you know. I'm a no-good piece of crap and …"

Mason blew out a sigh. "Please don't tell me you made the decision for her?"

"There was no decision to be made. Some guy she'd known for less than two weeks, or her dad?" Chance shook his head. "Even you can see how that had to go down."

"No. I don't see it. You should have let her decide for herself. I'm guessing you just walked straight out the door and she never even knew what went down, right?"

Chance nodded.

"Damn, Chance! Why? Why didn't you stick around? Why didn't you try to work it out?"

"Because the last thing her dad texted her was *We've come so far in the last few years. Don't throw it away over some no-good ranch hand.*" Mason met his gaze. "What else do you think he'd call you?"

Chance blew out an exasperated sigh. "Dammit, Mase. It's not about what he called me. I don't care what he called me. What I care about is that for him to say that—'we've come so far in the last few years'—then things haven't always been good between them, but they are now. I know how that feels. You know how many years I lost with my own dad. I'd hate for something to come between us, and I'm not going to be the thing that comes between Hope and her dad. It's better that she thinks I'm just an asshole who walked out on her in the middle of the night. Her dad can be the hero who picks up the pieces—and who was right about me. It's more important to me that she should be happy, than that she should be with me."

Mason shook his head but didn't say anything.

"What? Say it. Whatever you're thinking, just tell me."

"It doesn't matter what I'm thinking. It's your decision, and you already made it; but since you're asking, I think you're wrong. I think it was her choice to make and you should have let her."

Chance shrugged. He'd been beating himself up over that ever since he drove away from her house that night. "Maybe so, but like you said, it was my decision. I made it, and there's no going back now."

Mason raised an eyebrow. "There's not? Are you sure about that?"

Chance nodded. "Damned sure." He wasn't one to go back, but more than that, he couldn't allow his mind to open up to Hope again. He had to shut himself down—forget her and get on with his life.

"Why?"

"Because I can't. I can't do it to her and I can't do it to myself. Like I said, it no doubt wouldn't have worked out between us anyway. She lives in LA; she has a life and a business there. I live here and have," he smirked, "you and a bunch of cows to think about. We live different lives; it just wouldn't have worked. I just shaved a couple of months off the process of us figuring that out."

"If you say so."

"I say so. Has that answered all your questions? Can we leave it alone now?"

"Yeah."

Chance watched Mason's face, knowing there was still something else. "What? You may as well just go ahead and ask so we can close the subject once and for all."

"Okay. I will. I'm just wondering. You said she made you feel. Like you haven't since Chloe."

Chance pressed his lips together and nodded.

"Do you think that it was the right time, that you're ready to feel again now, and another woman might have made you feel that way, too? Or do you think it was her?"

Chance sighed. "Honestly, I've been trying to convince myself that it was just the timing. You know, right after I decided I need to start living again, I found Hope."

Mason nodded and waited.

"I have to believe that it was just the timing."

Mason nodded again and met his gaze.

Chance looked away.

"But it was more than that, wasn't it?"

Chance shrugged.

"If you ask me, you're a fool."

"I didn't ask you, though, did I?"

Chapter Two

Hope carried the tray out onto the terrace and placed it on the table in front of Toby with a smile.

"Thanks, that looks great."

"I need to feel useful somehow, and it seems making lunch is about all I'm good for these days."

Toby frowned at her. "So, come back into the office. Get back to work."

"I don't see the point. I finally understood while we were away that things run just as smoothly—if not more so—without me."

"Would you stop feeling sorry for yourself? I've been patient. I've tried being understanding, I've tried being gentle, but I think it's time for me to start kicking your butt."

Hope looked up and met his gaze. "Why?"

"Because I've never seen you like this before. You're the one who gets things done. You're a go-getter, not a sit-around-and-moper. I don't like seeing you like this. It's time for you to snap out of it. Do something."

She shrugged. "I know. You're right. I just don't know what to do. There's nothing I want to do."

"We both know that's a lie."

She nodded sadly. "Yes, we do, but you also know what I mean. I can't do any of the things I want to do."

"Why not?"

She shrugged. "You know what I want to do. I want to get in touch with Chance. I want to ask him what happened, what changed."

"So, why don't you do that? Put yourself out of your misery."

"Because the way he left made it quite clear. He's done. He doesn't want to see me anymore. End of story. Asking him to explain it to me is pointless. It'd just make him uncomfortable, and it'd make me feel even more stupid than I already do."

"Then I guess you just have to forget about it. Forget about him."

She nodded again. "I know, but for some reason, I can't. I keep turning it all over and over in my mind."

"Because you've got nothing else on your mind. You need to be busy. You need to get back to work, or at least back to play. If you don't want to come back to the office then at least get out and have some fun."

"I don't feel like it, though."

"I know, and that worries me. It's all the more reason that you should."

"Maybe next week."

Toby shook his head. "How about tomorrow night?"

"I don't think so."

"Please, Hope? I'd like you to be my plus one."

She narrowed her eyes at him. It was a habit she'd picked up from Chance. She knew from being on the receiving end of that look that it made you feel as though you had to answer the question—even though no question had been spoken. It worked.

"There's a big party for Sirena's birthday and I ..."

"You don't want to go by yourself?"

Toby nodded.

Hope had to smile. "You don't want to go by yourself, but you don't want to take anyone who could be mistaken for a real date."

Toby smiled. "Yeah, so you see you're my only Hope."

She closed her eyes briefly, not wanting to remember when Chance had spoken those same words to her. "It's a bit sneaky of you, don't you think?" He raised an eyebrow innocently, and she had to laugh. "You know full well that if it were just for me, I wouldn't go, but because it's for you, I kind of have to, don't I?"

"You don't have to."

"But I'll feel awful if I don't. So, I'll do it."

"Thanks and you never know, it might help. You need to take your mind off Chance. And ..."

"And what?"

"Sorry, but I'm going to say it. If you're not going to do anything about him, then you need to forget him and move on."

Hope pressed her lips together. It seemed she'd picked up more of Chance's mannerisms than she'd realized.

"Don't look at me like that! You're the realistic one. You're the one who looks for solutions, who gets things done. You know I'm right. You either do something about it, or you forget about it. Continuing to sit around here feeling sorry for yourself isn't a viable option. Not for you. It doesn't suit you."

She sighed. "I know. Thanks, Toby."

He smiled encouragingly. "Tomorrow night is a good start, it'll get you out and," he glanced at her sweatpants and baggy T-shirt, "get you back into grown-up clothes."

She laughed. "Watch it. I can still say no if you're going to start insulting me."

"I'm not insulting you, I'm teasing you, and hopefully appealing to your inner designer, who I can only assume is being held hostage while you've been possessed by an outer slob."

This time she didn't laugh. "Slob? That's going a bit far, isn't it?"

Toby gave her a stern look. "Have you looked in the mirror lately?"

She shook her head, realizing that she really hadn't paid any attention to her appearance or to much of anything, these last few weeks.

"Well, I suggest you don't, not until you've spent a day at the spa."

She laughed. "Am I that bad?"

"No, not really. I'm just trying to use shock tactics to snap you out of it."

"Well, it's working." She pulled the end of her ponytail around so she could look at it. Her hair needed washing.

"Yep, I suggest a cut and color, too," said Toby with a smile.

She sighed. "I guess your plan is working. I have a lot to do if I'm going to look presentable by tomorrow night, huh?"

He nodded. "Do you want me to fix your appointments?"

"No, thanks. I should get on it myself. You're right. It's time to get my butt into gear and stop slobbing around. Time to try and look halfway decent again."

Toby shook his head. "You're still beautiful, and you know it. It's only your grooming that's letting you down."

She sighed. "Why is it that even the word grooming makes me think about him? You groom horses. Chance rides horses. He loves horses." She met Toby's gaze. "We had such a wonderful afternoon out riding horses on the beach in Oregon."

Toby nodded sadly. "But you refuse to contact Chance, so there's no point raking it all over. Is there?"

"I can't contact him. He made it perfectly clear we were done. He even said he was sorry. I have to respect his choice. What else can I do? What am I supposed to do? What would you do?"

Toby shrugged. "If I were in your situation I don't think I could be as accepting as you are. I think I'd be demanding an explanation—either that or I'd be making some big, dumb gesture that would either win them over or kill any remaining chance I had by convincing them that I'm a crazy person."

Hope smiled as she thought that over. "What kind of big, crazy gesture?"

"Like I said, knowing me, it'd be a dumb one! Don't take anything I say as advice, will you? You know I'm no good at this kind of thing. Hell, I'm making you go with me to a birthday party for a woman I've admired from afar for the last year!" He stopped talking and gave her a puzzled look. "What? What are you thinking? Whatever it is, it's probably a really bad idea if it was inspired by anything I said."

She smiled. "I think it's a really good idea—to make a big gesture. It's sure to decide things one way or another. Either he'll love it and at least talk to me, or he'll think I'm a crazy stalker lady and tell me as much. Even if he does think I'm crazy, he'll tell me, and I'll have no choice but to give up. And at least I'll know I tried, that I didn't just meekly accept that it was all over without even trying for a second chance."

Toby looked wary. "And do you know what kind of big gesture you have in mind?"

She smiled; she did. It was perfect. "I do, but I need to find out if it's going to be possible first." She got up from the table and went back inside.

Toby followed her. "So, is this it? Am I dismissed for the afternoon, now?"

She laughed. "You're the one who suddenly filled my day with a bunch of things I need to get done. And besides, don't you want to go shopping and find the perfect gift for Sirena?"

Toby's eyes widened. "What do you think I should get her?"

Hope laughed. "Maybe you should go for some big gesture?"

He rolled his eyes. "You know me better than that. I'll spout that kind of thing when it's just talk, but when it comes to her I'm a total coward."

"You are. I've never understood that one. I'll have a think and call you if I come up with any ideas."

"Thanks."

~ ~ ~

Chance grabbed his hat from the hook on the door and picked up his keys. He needed to get out. He didn't know where he was going, but he had to go somewhere. His chat with Mason this morning hadn't helped at all. It had made him feel worse. Was Mason right? Was he a fool? Should he have talked to Hope before he left Oregon the way he did? He strode over to his truck and climbed in. What did it matter? Right or wrong, what was done was done. He needed to just stick with what he'd been trying to do ever since he left her that note and closed the door behind him. He needed to put her out of his mind. Forget her. He pointed the truck up the driveway and headed out. He sighed when he saw a figure waving at him up by the guest ranch. Shane. Chance wasn't in the mood for him today. Shane was relentlessly upbeat, and that wasn't what he needed to deal with. He pulled over reluctantly and forced a smile.

"Where are you off to?" asked Shane with a grin.

"I'm heading up to town. I need to go to the post office." Chance was surprised how easily that came out. He hadn't had any intention of going to town until he said it.

"It's good to see you going somewhere."

"And what does that mean?"

He felt bad at the way Shane's grin faltered. "Nothing. It's just you haven't been out and about much since you came back. You've either been working even longer hours than usual or holed up in the cabin like some kind of vampire." His grin returned. "Sorry, I can't help it. Cassidy's been trying to teach me that I'm not the center of the universe and that I need to pay attention to how other people are feeling." He shrugged. "Even I know you're not in a good place. Consider this my half-assed attempt to show that I care—even if I don't know what to do."

Chance couldn't help smiling. "Thanks, Shane. I didn't mean to bite your head off. I'm okay."

Shane grinned again. "Which means you're not okay, and you don't want to talk about it, right?"

Chance chuckled. "Yep. She's teaching you well."

Shane laughed with him. "Can I tell her you said that?"

"Sure."

"Are you doing anything tonight?"

"No."

Shane held up a hand. "It's okay. I know you don't want to talk about your troubles or anything, but Cassidy's up in town tonight with her seniors from the art class. Can I come hang with you? We could grill some burgers and drink some beers, like old times?"

Chance was about to say no, but he thought about it. Shane was easy company. He, Chance, and Mason had all lived in the cabin together until not so long ago. Until they'd met Cassidy and Gina. No, that line of thought was making him think about Hope again. That made his decision for him; having Shane over would sure beat sitting there staring at the wall thinking about Hope. "Yeah, why not?"

"Great. Give me a shout when you get back from town, and I'll come over."

"Okay. See you later."

Chance pulled out of the driveway and headed north up East River Road toward town. It was a beautiful day. The sun was shining in a big, blue sky. The mountains still wore their snowy caps, but the foothills were already tinged with green. The river was rushing, swollen with the spring run-off. He sighed. He was trying to focus on the everyday details of the landscape to keep his mind away from Hope. It wasn't working. The blue sky reminded him of their ride on the beach; they'd been so lucky to get a cloud-free afternoon for that. The green reminded him of everything about Oregon, how lush everything was there. He shook his head. Why was it so hard not to think about her? He felt a pang of guilt at the realization that he thought about her so much, he'd hardly thought about Chloe at all. There wasn't normally a day that went by that he didn't think about Chloe, some moment that he wanted to share with her, or something that triggered a memory of her. In the month since he'd been back in the valley, it hadn't been the same. Now everything reminded him of Hope. How screwed up was he? It had taken him eighteen years before he let himself get close to another woman, and when he did, he'd cut things off with her before they could even get started.

When he got to town, he pulled up across the road from the post office and then wondered what the hell he was doing there. He'd told Shane this was where he was going, but he had no reason to. He felt pretty dumb. He'd made the half hour drive up here for nothing. He should buy some stamps at least, so it wasn't a completely wasted trip. He climbed out of the truck and crossed the road.

His heart began to race in his chest when he saw the door open and a familiar figure come out. Dr. Johnny. Chance looked around wildly, hoping for an escape. Could he run and hide behind a parked truck before Johnny saw him? No.

"Chance!"

He forced a smile and stepped forward to shake Johnny's outstretched hand. "This is a pleasant surprise. How are you? How's your father getting along?"

"It is a surprise!" Chance hadn't expected to see him back up here until the summer. "Dad's doing great, thanks to you. The clinic was the best thing that's happened to him."

"The clinic just provided the tools and the environment. Your father did all the hard work. He's a great example of what's possible with determination and the right attitude."

Chance nodded. "Yeah, he sure has those. I talk to him most days, and even according to him he's doing great." He smiled. "According to Alice and my sister, he's overdoing it."

"That doesn't surprise me in the least. And how about you?"

Chance tried to ignore the concern in his eyes. "Yeah, I'm fine thanks. It's back to the grind for me."

Johnny nodded. "I hope the time you spent in Oregon was good for you?"

Chance nodded, not sure what the question meant or how to answer it. Was Johnny really asking about him and Hope, or was he just being hypersensitive?

"Is there any chance of you taking another break any time soon?"

"No. Like I said, it's back to the grindstone now."

Johnny met his gaze. "That's a shame. I might as well tell you; I was keeping my fingers crossed for you and Hope."

Chance sucked in a deep breath, surprised that he would just come straight out and say it like that.

"I know it's none of my business, but I hoped, you know."

Chance liked the older man; he hated to feel that he'd disappointed him somehow. "I did, too. She's an amazing lady, but it's not realistic, is it? She lives there; I live here. She's who she is. I'm just … I run cattle."

"I suppose on the surface those things might be enough to stop the two of you, but I didn't think they would."

Chance shrugged. "It's better for her this way."

Johnny gave him a stern look that surprised him. It almost felt as though he knew what had happened. His words reinforced that feeling. "Does she think that?"

Chance stared at him. "I'm sure she does."

Johnny grasped his shoulder. "It's not my place to say anything, is it?"

Chance shook his head but didn't want to agree out loud. "Do you mind if I ask you something, though?"

"What's that?"

"You seem disappointed that we didn't work it out. I thought you'd be relieved."

Johnny looked genuinely puzzled and waited for him to explain.

"I mean,- I would have thought that in your eyes she deserves better."

Johnny let out a short laugh. "In my eyes, there is no one better than you, Chance. I don't measure a person's worth in dollars if that's what you mean."

"That and the, I don't even know what you call it, the social standing, I guess. I'm not a millionaire, and worse than that I'm a no-name non-millionaire."

Johnny laughed again. "I know what you mean, Chance, but I'm not that shallow, and I think you already know Hope isn't."

Chance nodded. "Sorry, I do, but," he had to ask, "what about her father?"

Johnny's smile faded. "Seymour isn't shallow, but let's say he does observe certain social norms. However, he's good at understanding a person's true worth when he meets them." He held Chance's gaze. "It's a pity you never met him."

It sure did seem that he knew what happened between him and Hope.

"Anyway. It's good to run into you, Chance. I hope I'll see you again. I'm going to be here for the rest of the month."

"Be sure and give me a call if you need anything."

"Thanks. I might just do that. Bye now."

As he started to walk away, Chance tried to bite his tongue, but he couldn't help it. "Dr. Johnny!"

He turned and looked back.

"How is she?"

Johnny smiled. "I wish you'd ask her that yourself. From what I've seen she's not doing wonderfully." He turned around and walked away.

Chance stood staring after him for a long time. What did that mean? Johnny thought he should ask her himself? Did that mean she'd want him to call her? She wasn't doing wonderfully? Did that mean she was upset about the way he'd left Oregon? He crossed the road again and got back in his truck. What the hell? What was he supposed to do now? How was he supposed to forget her now?

Chapter Three

Hope checked herself over in the mirror while she waited for the car to arrive. She smiled; this should prove Toby wrong about her having devolved into a slob! Since he'd left here yesterday afternoon she'd been on a whirlwind of beautification appointments. She'd had a mani-pedi while her hair was being cut and colored. She'd had a deep tissue massage and a rejuvenating facial. And wax—she peered more closely at her eyebrows in the mirror. Yes, all the redness was gone now, though other parts of her still felt a little tender. Someday she'd make time to get laser treatment on every single undesirable follicle on her body—and never have to face the torture of waxing ever again! Her brows and lashes were tinted, her makeup was perfect, if she did say so herself, and this dress! Wow! It was a white satin number she'd picked up this morning during a little bout of retail therapy. She smiled at the way her hair curled down around her shoulders and brushed a strand away from her face. Her smile faded as she remembered Chance doing the same thing while they sat on the patio overlooking the beach. She closed her eyes, remembering the way his roughened fingertips had traced her cheek so gently. No. She opened them again. She was supposed to be dragging herself out of her funk over him. She couldn't go indulging in all the sweet memories and sink back down into misery again. She straightened her shoulders. Like Toby had said she had to do something about it, or forget about it. She was leaning toward doing something, but until she did, she was no longer prepared to let herself wallow.

She looked up at the sound of a car coming up the driveway and picked up her purse. Toby's timing was great. No wallowing, not even for a few minutes. It was time to go out and have some fun. She opened the front door and laughed at the look on his face as he got out of the car.

"Wow! You have been busy. You look amazing."

"Thanks." She trotted down the front steps to join him. He held the rear door open for her and then came around to sit beside her.

The driver turned around to smile at her. "It's good to see you out and about Miss Hope, and if you don't mind me saying, you look great!"

She smiled and touched his shoulder. "Thanks, Ron. Toby here told me I was turning into a slob, so I thought I'd better make a bit of an effort."

Ron turned a dark look on Toby. "I'd say Toby needs to watch his mouth, or he'll have me to answer to."

They all laughed. Ron had been driving for her for years and there was usually some kind of teasing and banter between the three of them.

Toby shrugged. "You didn't see her yesterday."

"He's right, Ron. Much as I hate to admit it, I had let myself go. We can forgive him this time, because he gave me the boost I needed to remind him just how unsloblike I really am!"

"If you say so, Miss Hope, but I've got my eye on you, Toby, you'd best remember that."

Toby laughed. "You never let me forget it!"

Ron pulled out of the driveway and smiled at them in the rearview mirror.

"Do you know who's going to be there tonight?" she asked Toby.

"Just about everyone, by the sound of it. Sirena's mom organized the party and it seems she's invited absolutely everyone who's anyone."

Hope raised an eyebrow. "Is Drew going to be there?"

"I wouldn't do that to you. That was the first thing I checked on. Apparently, he was invited, but he's out of town. He's meeting with some producer in New York. For once I wish him the best of luck."

"What do you mean?"

"I mean I hope he gets a part in whatever movie it is. If he had to go to New York just to talk about it, then I doubt they'll be filming here in LA."

Hope nodded. "I guess not. I don't really care though. It doesn't matter to me anymore."

Up front, Ron coughed and muttered "Asshole," under his breath.

Hope laughed. "We haven't talked much since then, have we, Ron? I don't suppose you were too sorry to see him go?"

Ron chuckled. "I think I just made my feelings on the matter clear. I don't know what you saw in him, but I'm glad you've seen the back of him."

"Yeah, me too."

The traffic wasn't too bad this evening and before long they were pulling up in front of the club. Ron gave her a kind smile when she got out. "You call me when you've had enough, won't you? I can whisk you away home if you're tired and come back for this fella later."

Hope reached up and kissed his cheek. "Thanks, Ron. I think I'll be okay. You're too good me."

He nodded and held her gaze for a moment. "I just look out for you, that's all."

Toby came around to join them and took Hope's arm with a grin. "Would you stop kissing on Ron? You're supposed to be my date. What will people think?"

Ron laughed. "They'll think she's got good taste and went for the better man."

Toby rolled his eyes. "They probably will!"

"Come on, we'd better get in there. I'll call you ten minutes before we need you, Ron."

He smiled. "I'll be ready the second you call."

Once they were inside, Hope looked around with a smile. She was glad she'd come. There were so many familiar faces milling around. It'd do her good to catch up with acquaintances. It'd do her good to show her face around town again. The way things had worked out, she hadn't been seen out in public since the Drew fiasco. People were probably thinking she was devastated and was lying low. They'd be right, of course—over everything except the guy involved.

Alana Mills, Sirena's mother, glided toward them with a welcoming smile on her face. Hope loved her; she was a real sweetie.

"Hope, darling! I'm so glad you're here. I wasn't sure you'd feel up to it."

"I'm feeling fine thanks, Mrs. Mills. Thanks for inviting me."

"And me," added Toby.

Mrs. Mills smiled at him, "You're welcome, dear."

Hope felt bad. She saw Toby as a friend and an equal, too many people in their circle saw him as nothing more than her assistant. "Do you know where Sirena is?" she asked. "We'd love to say happy birthday."

"Of course, she's out on the garden terrace. I'll show you through."

"That's okay, thanks. We know the way. Thanks again for inviting us, I'm sure we'll catch up with you later." Hope led Toby away before the older woman had chance to answer.

Toby sighed as they made their way through the crowds, smiling and waving at the other guests, but never slowing enough to get caught in conversation. "What are you doing, Hope? You know I'm not just going to march up to her and wish her happy birthday."

"I do, but I don't know why. You're a dumbass when it comes to Sirena."

"Yup. I admit it. I am. But you're not going to change it, and you certainly won't change it by embarrassing me and making me talk to her."

Hope laughed. "I know! Stop worrying, would you? I'm going to march straight up to her and say Happy Birthday."

"But you don't even know her that well."

Hope shrugged. "That doesn't matter. There are some perks to being a Davenport. I might not be a close friend, but I know her mom and she knows who I am. That's all we need to start up a conversation. All you need to do is stand there and look handsome."

Toby rolled his eyes.

"There she is. Come on." Hope led him across the patio to where Sirena was sitting with a small group of friends. She stopped a little distance away and waited for a break in the conversation. She might have claimed that she was about to march straight up to her, but she didn't work that way. She didn't need to, as Sirena proved when she spotted her. She stopped talking and smiled at them. Hope seized her moment. "I'm sorry. I don't mean to intrude." Toby squeezed her arm tighter—no doubt meaning, _yes you did!_

Sirena looked a little surprised, but covered it quickly. "Oh, that's okay. Join us, if you'd like."

"Thank you. We wanted to come wish you a very happy birthday." She dragged Toby with her and took a seat on one end of a loveseat, leaving Toby to sit on the end closest to Sirena.

"Yes, happy birthday," he mumbled.

Hope was happy to see the tiniest hint of pink flush Sirena's cheeks as she muttered thank you. Perhaps there was a chance for these two after all? She waited a moment, but neither of them spoke, so she decided to jump in and get the conversation going before she left them to it. "I'm so glad you invited me. I haven't been out for a while."

Sirena met her gaze. "I wasn't sure if you'd come. Are you okay?"

That surprised Hope. Normally in these circles, people spoke in riddles and never actually said what they meant, they just alluded to it. Sirena's approach was refreshing. She smiled. "I am, thanks. I think it all worked out for the best."

"That's good to hear." Sirena looked at her friends. "Would you mind going to get me another drink, Ellie?" Ellie seemed to understand the unspoken request to leave them alone and nodded. "Come on Kara, you can help me." They got to their feet and the others joined them, leaving Hope, Toby and Sirena alone.

Hope wanted to slap Toby when he sniffed at his armpit and asked, "Do I need a new deodorant?" Why would he blow his chance like that? She was surprised to hear Sirena laughing. Wow! Everyone's humor was different, she supposed.

"It's okay. It's not you," said Sirena. "I just wanted to get you alone for a moment, Hope. I wanted to let you know that Drew won't be here tonight. Mom invited him—against my wishes—but he couldn't make it."

"Thanks for letting me know. I really am okay about it, but I can relax a little more knowing that I'm not going to run into him."

Sirena looked uncomfortable. "I don't know how relaxed you'll be when I tell you that Carrie might come, though. I'm sorry. I really didn't think you'd show up, and Carrie's been down in the dumps since she discovered what Drew's really like."

Hope raised an eyebrow. "They're not together anymore?"

Sirena shook her head. "I know you must hate her—"

"Not at all. If anything, I feel a little sorry for her, hearing that."

Sirena smiled. "You're such a class act."

"Thank you! That's a lovely thing to say."

"It's a lovely way to be. I think you're awesome!" Sirena looked embarrassed when she blurted that out.

"That's okay, I think she's awesome, too." Toby was no doubt trying to make her feel better, but it seemed to have the opposite effect.

Sirena's face fell. "Are the two of you together now?"

Hope looked at Toby who met her gaze with an incredulous look before they both burst out laughing. "Oh, my goodness, we're not! We work together, but that's it."

"Oh!" From the way Sirena's eyes lit up, Hope would guess that all Toby needed to do was get his act together and ask her out. "I thought you were …"

"No," said Toby. Hope willed him not to say anything stupid and ruin his chances. "I'm just the guy who holds everything together. You know, the behind the scenes guy who everyone appreciates but no one wants to be with?"

"I'd love to be with a guy a like that," said Sirena. "It seems these days everyone's trying to be a badass and no one wants to be a down to earth genuine person."

Hope grinned. "Oh, I think you two should talk!"

Toby gave her the rabbit in the headlights look, but Sirena smiled gratefully. They'd be fine, she knew it.

"I have so many people to catch up with. I'll check back on you later."

"Thanks," said Sirena as Hope got up.

Toby gave her another look of wild eyed panic. She smiled to herself. He needed to step up, he'd do better once she was out of the way. He always came through under pressure. "See you later," she told him with a grin.

Hope wandered over to a quiet corner of the patio. She should catch up with people, but she really didn't feel like it. If she was lucky, she might be able to catch a waiter's attention and get them to bring a drink over to her hideout in the foliage. She leaned against a planter and watched people mingle. There were so many familiar faces, yet so few friends amongst them. She had acquaintances by the boatload, but she didn't really have any real friends. She smiled to herself sadly. Toby was as close as it got—and she paid him! That wasn't fair, he was a good friend, and she had no doubt he still would be, even if their working relationship were to end.

A waiter approached with a tray of champagne glasses. She took one gratefully, and then swiped a second—it could legitimately be for a friend. She felt a little guilty knocking back the first one while clutching the second in her other hand. She'd just have to hope that no one took a picture of her like that. They'd no doubt claim she was drowning her sorrows two drinks at a time. She chuckled to herself as she slipped the empty glass into the planter.

"I had a feeling they were both for you."

She looked up with a polite smile, trying to mask her guilt. "I'm sorry?"

The guy smiled. "That's okay. I didn't see a thing."

She smiled back; there was something about him that told her he was okay. She didn't know him, but he seemed familiar somehow.

He called the waiter over and took two glasses of champagne, then winked at her. "You should probably take two as well, the others will be back any minute."

She smiled through pursed lips as she took two glasses and then laughed with him as the waiter walked away. "I don't have a drinking problem," she said with a smile.

"It doesn't look like it. You're getting your hands on all the bubbly you want. No problem at all."

She chuckled. She felt immediately at ease with this guy, though she didn't know why. He seemed familiar, and comfortable. She put one of her glasses down and held out her hand. "I'm Hope Davenport, nice to meet you."

The guy grinned. It looked like it was a well-practiced sexy grin. Oh, no! He wasn't trying to pick her up, was he? "You don't know me, do you?"

She tried not to let her smile slip, but she was starting to feel a little uneasy now. Was she walking into some kind of ambush here? "I'm sorry, I don't. Should I?"

He laughed, and her tension dissolved. "No, you shouldn't. I guess I'm just getting a bit too big for my boots lately." He shook her hand firmly. "I apologize, ma'am. I'm Matt McLellan. Just a humble country boy, who sings a couple of songs."

"Oh!" She did know him. She loved his music! How had she not recognized him? Probably because he wasn't wearing his trademark cowboy hat. "I'm sorry, Matt. I didn't recognize you. Of course, I know you. I'm so sorry, it's probably just seeing you out of context like this."

"Hey, no need to apologize. I'm the one who landed myself on you. There's no reason you should know me."

She smiled, starting to relax again. "I love your music. I'm glad you came to introduce yourself." She raised her glass to him. "And to have a drink with me."

"I hate to see a lady drink alone."

She nodded.

"I think women only drink alone when they're sad, and I hope you're not sad?"

Uh-oh, was this a roundabout way of getting to a pickup? She hoped not. "I'm fine, thank you." she couldn't manage to keep the hard edge out of her voice.

"Jeez! I'm a dumb son of a gun. I ain't hitting on you. I'm sorry. I should explain, see, what it is, is that I saw you and Chance together, in the news, about a month back. I was so damned happy for him. If anyone deserves to be happy, it's that guy. But then I didn't see anything else about the two of you. Not till I see you here drinking alone. It's none of my business and I know it, but Chance is a friend, and—"

"You're his friend?"

Matt looked a little uncomfortable. "Well, that might be stretching it a bit. I met him. We helped each other out of a tight spot once. I owe him. Even though he says he owes me. He's a good guy." He met her gaze looking a little shame faced. "It's none of my damned business. I know. It's just when I saw you, I wanted to know. And ..." He waved his glass at all the people around them. "This isn't exactly my crowd. I thought since you and Chance got along you mustn't be a snooty—I mean, you must be nice. And ... Shall I just shut up and go away? Every time I open my mouth I make it worse, don't I?"

Hope had to laugh. "No. Don't go away. Please. I know what you mean."

"Phew! And there I thought I'd blown it."

"You did your best, but I'm quite understanding."

Matt laughed. "And you say it like you see it, right?"

She nodded, aware suddenly of the looks that were coming their way. She knew what people were assuming, and much as she'd like to talk to Matt, she didn't need that kind of attention. "How long are you in town for?" she asked.

"Till next Thursday."

She smiled. "I have to leave now, but could we meet up for lunch one day?"

Matt grinned. "Sure thing."

Hope pulled out her phone and called Ron. "Please, can we go home soon?"

"I'll be outside the front door in two minutes."

"Thanks, Ron. You're the best."

She looked at Matt. "Can I have your number?" She tapped it into her phone as he said it. "Thanks. I'll call you."

"I'll look forward to it."

Hope walked by the spot where she'd left Toby and Sirena, but there was no sign of them. She hoped he was okay. She needn't have worried, she spotted them on the dancefloor as she made her way out through the bar. Good for him, maybe tonight had been the little push Toby had needed.

Ron was standing by the car when she got outside. He opened the door and saw her safely inside before running back around to the driver's side and pulling away in a hurry.

"Is everything okay?"

"It's fine, thanks, Ron. I'd just had enough. It was my first trip out in a while and I don't need to stay for hours."

"No, you take your time, ease yourself back in gently."

Hope nodded. She wouldn't have minded staying. She would have loved to talk to Matt and found out how he knew Chance—and what he knew about Chance, whether he was okay. But it wasn't worth it. Too many pairs of eyes had turned their way once they'd been talking for more than a few minutes. The last thing she wanted was any rumors starting about the two of them. She'd had more than enough media attention lately.

Chapter Four

Chance sat on the back porch sipping a beer and watching the mountains while he waited for the grill to heat up. Seeing Johnny this afternoon had set him back even further than his chat with Mason had this morning. He jumped when Shane appeared around the side of the cabin.

"Damn. You must have been a million miles away, I can never normally sneak up on you," Shane said with a grin.

Chance scowled, hating that he'd been caught off guard like that. Shane was right, it wasn't like him. "What do you want?"

Shane rolled his eyes. "I thought you were going to call me when you got back from town. It's getting late so I decided to just stop by and see if you were here." He eyed the grill and the beer in Chance's hand. "I can beat feet and leave you to it, if you want. You should have just said if you didn't want the company."

Chance blew out a sigh and smiled. "Sorry. It totally slipped my mind." He stood up. "I'll go get you a cold one."

"I'll get it myself and bring you a fresh one. I'll feel less like a visitor then."

"Okay, have at it." He smiled to himself when Shane went inside. This place had been his home for a number of years, too.

When Shane came back out, he handed him a fresh beer and sat down on one of the rockers. He popped the top of his own beer and raised it to Chance. "Here's to …" He frowned. "I dunno. Here's to two old buddies sitting on the porch and shooting the shit."

Chance laughed and tapped his bottle against Shane's. "I'll drink to that."

"Good, I was afraid that anything I said might be something you didn't want to drink to at the moment."

"Yeah, so was I, but sitting on the porch and drinking a beer is just fine by me."

"Good. I'm guessing you don't want to talk about anything heavy."

Chance shook his head. "Nah. It's been a heavy day already."

Shane nodded and stared out at the mountains. They sat in companionable silence for a while until the grill was hot. Chance made them a couple of burgers and they fell back into the old routine they'd shared for years. Shane went back and forth to the kitchen, bringing plates out and getting the little table set up with ketchup and more beers while Chance was in charge of the grill.

When they sat down to eat, he smiled. "We make a good team, huh?"

Shane laughed. "I was just thinking, we're like an old married couple."

"I wouldn't go that far."

"Oh. Sorry. I didn't mean…"

Chance shook his head. "Don't worry. I'm not that sensitive. I just mean that … hell, I don't even know what I meant. I was going to make some joke about married couples bickering and bossing each other around, but that's just an old stereotype, isn't it? Your mom and dad aren't like that. You and Cassidy aren't."

Shane laughed. "I don't know. We don't bicker much, but she's pretty bossy."

Chance laughed with him. "She's not bossy. She's assertive, and you love that about her."

"I do. She's awesome. I still can't believe that we're married, and it's all going so well." His smile faded. "Shit, I'm sorry. I feel like everything I say is rubbing your nose in the fact that I'm happy and you're not."

"It's not like that, though, is it? You are happy. You shouldn't have to hide that just because I'm a mess. And you're not giving me enough credit anyway."

"How?"

Chance smiled. "I might be a mess, but I'm happy for you. I love seeing you and all the others happy. You deserve it."

"But so do you."

Chance shrugged. "Maybe, then again, maybe I don't."

Shane scowled at him. "Don't give me that shit. Please, tell me you're not going down that road? You're not starting to think that you don't deserve happiness, and that you'll never be happy, are you?"

"No, I'm not starting to think that. I've always thought that. I've believed that ever since Chloe died. My chance at happiness died with her. That's what I've lived my life believing, right up until six weeks ago."

Shane's eyes grew wide and he swallowed his mouthful of burger with a big gulping sound.

Chance nodded. "Keep it zipped and yes, I will tell you what I mean. It seems I need to talk, even though I don't really want to."

Shane nodded and took another big bite of burger, making clear that his mouth was full and he wouldn't be interrupting.

"I can't believe it's only been six weeks. It seems like so much longer since I found Hope."

Shane stopped chewing and waited for him to continue.

"She's," he blew out a sigh, "she's amazing. She's strong and smart. She reminds me of Cassidy in some ways. But not totally. She's confident, and she gets things done, but she's softer." Shane frowned, making him smile. "I'm not saying Cassidy's not soft, but she's tough. Cassidy's tough all the way through. Hope is tough on the outside, but she ... I don't know. The point is, she made me feel that maybe I could be happy. She made me think that maybe I've had it wrong all these years. It wasn't life that decided I could never be happy after Chloe. Maybe it was me who decided that I couldn't be happy—and blamed life for it." He shook his head. Apparently, it did help to talk; until he'd said that out loud, he hadn't totally understood it. He met Shane's gaze. "So, there I was starting to believe again, and life goes and pulls the rug out from under my feet a second time."

Shane nodded, but didn't say anything.

Chance met his gaze, surprised to realize that he was waiting to hear what he had to say.

"What? I'm here to listen, not to mess up by saying the wrong thing."

Chance smiled. "I don't think there is a right or wrong thing to say. I'm just curious to hear what you think."

"Okay, if you're sure?"

"I'm sure."

Shane smiled. "You can understand me being wary, you've shot me down enough times in the past."

Chance nodded. "I won't shoot you down this time."

"Well, I can see where you're coming from, but one thing surprises me."

"What's that?"

"It surprises me that you're giving up so easily."

Chance frowned. "I'm not giving up."

Shane raised an eyebrow. "Are you going to shoot me down, or let me talk?"

Chance pressed his lips together.

"Thank you. You can argue with me when I'm done, if you like, but you asked what I think so here it is. You say you realized that life hadn't done anything to you, that you'd decided for yourself that you couldn't be happy. You took responsibility. Now you've been knocked down again by whatever happened between you and Hope, and instead of sticking with the understanding that you're in charge of your own happiness, you've gone back to blaming life again. You're giving up. If it were anyone else, I'd go so far as to say they were acting like a victim." He gave Chance a wary smile. "But this is you, so I'm not going to say anything like that, but can you see where I'm coming from?"

Chance drew in a deep breath and nodded slowly. "I can. You really are more than just a pretty face, aren't you?"

Shane laughed.

Chance stared out at the mountains while he mulled over what Shane had just said. If it was true—if he really was making himself a victim ... He shook his head angrily at the thought. He didn't do that, that wasn't who he was—was it? But if that was what he was doing, what was the alternative? If he accepted that life didn't have it in for him, that he hadn't been dealt a hand that meant he could never be happy, then what? Then he had to make his own happiness, just like everyone else. And how could he do that? He looked at Shane who was watching him warily.

"You asked me to tell you."

Chance smiled. "I know, I just didn't expect to get such pearls of wisdom from you."

Shane chuckled. "I could either take that as an insult or a compliment. I'll go with compliment."

"Good, that's how it was intended, thank you. It's not easy to admit, but I think you're right. I'm not just a feather blown on the wind."

Shane laughed. "Damned straight you're not. You're more like a big-ass eagle flying wherever you want to go, soaring and swooping wherever you choose."

Chance laughed with him. "Pearls of wisdom and beautiful similes, too."

Shane frowned. "I thought it was a metaphor."

Chance grinned. "Never mind. The point is that you just gave me the kick up the ass I needed, and I appreciate it."

"Great. What are you going to do about it?"

"I dunno, yet."

Shane's smile faded. "You need to figure it out. Understanding is a wonderful thing, but if you never use it, it's pretty much worthless."

Chance nodded, wondering just how he could put his new understanding to good use.

"If you really do believe that you're in charge of your own happiness, what are you going to do about it? What do you think would make you happy?"

Chance shrugged.

Shane raised an eyebrow. "I'm probably going too far now, but is it fair to say that your new belief that happiness was possible was all tied up with Hope?"

Chance nodded.

"But for some reason you're not pursuing that?"

Chance shook his head.

"What did life do to you, that made you think it wasn't possible for you to be happy with her?"

Chance pressed his lips together. Did he really want to talk about it?

Shane waited; he didn't seem as ready to back down as he had been earlier. He was pushing him to come up with answers, and Chance loved him for it.

He blew out a sigh. "Okay. I'll tell you what happened."

Shane shook his head rapidly. "That's not what I'm after. I'm not trying to make you …"

"I know, you're trying to help me, but you can't understand if you don't know what happened. So, we spent our time together while we were in Oregon. We decided that we were going to give it a shot at carrying on seeing each other when we left there. She was going to come up here to see me."

Shane nodded sadly. "And then the press went and blew it for you."

"No! Well, yes, but it didn't affect us. We got through that just fine. But that last night we were there, her dad was texting her in the middle of the night saying he didn't want her to get involved with me. That he knew what I was—a criminal—and that they'd come a long way in the last few years and he didn't want her to throw that away over someone like me."

"But if he knew you, if he met you, he'd love you. I know that. Surely she could see it. Did she not even try to talk him around?"

Chance shook his head grimly.

"Oh. I get it. She would have talked him around if you'd let her, but you didn't. You decided to do the noble thing and bow out, right?"

"Don't say it like that. I did what was best for her and her relationship with her dad."

"What you thought was best, or what she thought was best?"

Chance shrugged.

"I thought as much." Shane shook his head. "I always knew you had issues, but man, have you got issues."

"And what does that mean?"

"It means that what I said before about you playing the victim was right on the money. You didn't fight for your chance at happiness, you didn't do anything except walk away when the going got tough, and now you're blaming life, saying that it doesn't want you to be happy. Can you see how screwed up that is?"

Chance stared at him for a long moment, waiting for his anger to simmer down. Part of him wanted to grab Shane, to make him apologize for calling him a coward. Another, more reasonable, part of him knew that Shane was right. He'd used the texts from Seymour Davenport as an excuse. An excuse to not take things any further with Hope, and to absolve himself of any responsibility by making out that he was doing the right thing—what was best for her.

Shane was glaring back at him, not prepared to back down at all this time. "You can be as mad as you like at me. I don't care. It's worth it, if I can wake you up to what you're doing. You're destroying your own life, and pretending there's nothing you can do about it."

Chance nodded slowly. "You're right. I hate it. I hate seeing it, I hate admitting it, but you are one hundred percent right."

Shane relaxed a little. "I hate that I'm right too, but you need to face it. You've done this to yourself."

"Yeah, I screwed up in a big way, huh?"

Shane smiled. "Yeah, but take it from one who knows. The one good thing about screwing up is that since you're the one who made the mess, you're also the one who can make it right again. With responsibility comes freedom. When you own your mistakes, you can make amends for them."

Chance laughed, glad to relieve a little of the tension. "Damn, Shane. If ever you decide to quit the hospitality business, I reckon you could do pretty well as a counselor."

Shane grinned. "If only Cassidy could hear you now."

"Yeah, I'll be sure to let her know just how awesome you are."

"Thanks. But, where does it leave you? What are you going to do? Is Hope your one and only chance at happiness, or was she just a wake up to the fact you can be happy?"

Chance shook his head slowly. "It's not about happiness, it's all about Hope."

"I thought as much. Any ideas what you're going to do?"

"Not yet, but thanks to you, I know I need to do something. I've spent the last month trying to shut myself down, to let it go, forget about her. Now I can finally admit that I don't want to do that. I just have to figure out what I can do."

Shane smiled. "It's a pity you didn't talk to me sooner, huh?"

"It is, but I probably wouldn't have heard what you had to say. I wasn't ready."

Shane swaggered his shoulders. "See, I'm not just smarter than the average bear, I also have great timing."

Chance laughed and stood up. "You do. And by way of a thank you, I'm going to break out the ice cream."

Shane laughed. "What, now I'm back to being the baby brother who gets ice cream as a reward for being a clever boy?"

Chance shook his head. "No, asshole. You're getting ice cream because I know you love it!"

"Aww." Shane winked at him. "Is the big bad Chancey going to write thank you in toffee sauce on my ice cream?"

Chance laughed and went inside. When he came back out, Shane was looking serious again. "You still haven't decided what you're going to do."

"I know."

"Can't you just call her, ask if you can talk?"

"No."

"You can't or you won't?"

"I can't. See, when I left her place for the last time, I deleted her number from my phone. You know, so that I wouldn't give in to temptation and call her after a day or two?"

"And you don't know anyone who could give you her number?"

"I do. Dr. Johnny. Her Uncle Johnny. I bumped into him in town today. He's going to be at his ranch for the next month.

Shane grinned. "So, call him. Ask for her number."

Chance shrugged. He didn't know how he felt about that. It should be easy. When Chance had asked him how Hope was this afternoon, Johnny had said he wished Chance would ask her himself.

"Coward!"

He had to smile. "Don't start pushing your luck."

Shane held both hands up. "I'm trying to push you into doing something—preferably something constructive and not something like punching me in the mouth!"

"Okay. I'll do it. I'll call him tomorrow."

Shane checked his watch. "It's not late."

"I said I'll do it tomorrow."

"Okay. Okay."

Chapter Five

"Are you ever going to come back into the office?"

Hope shrugged. "Probably. At some point. It's not like I'm needed for anything, is it?"

Toby sighed. "Only to run the business, to come up with new designs, to be our leader. Nothing much apart from that, no."

"Come on. You know full well that I'm not actually needed to do any of those things. Bill runs the business, and he always has. I was the face, the figurehead; he's always been the mastermind. Ariana and Celia are better designers than I'll ever be. They're young, and they're fresh, they have new ideas. We brought them in to move us forward, and they're doing exactly that."

"You're still the leader."

"I'm the figurehead."

"So, you're never coming back?"

"I didn't say that. I just don't want to at the moment. Anyway, I invited you over for dinner as a friend. Not to talk about work." They were sitting out on the terrace again. This seemed to be the only place she spent any time lately. They'd enjoyed a wonderful pasta and were now sharing an excellent bottle of wine. The wine that Chance had bought for her. It was that beautiful time in the evening when the sky glowed through oranges, purples, and blues before it went dark. The lights of the city twinkled against it.

"If you don't want to talk about work and you don't want to talk about Chance, what else is there to talk about?" The smile on his face told her there was a lot to talk about. She wanted to hear how his evening had gone when she'd left him with Sirena. He'd deliberately avoided the subject and had talked work, work, work all through dinner.

"You know what I want to talk about! Don't pretend you don't. I want to know how things went with you and Sirena, but if you're not prepared to tell me, I could always call her."

Toby's eyes widened. "You wouldn't!"

"I will if you don't tell me all about it right now."

He smiled. "We had a very nice time, thank you. We danced and we talked and we laughed."

"Did she laugh with you or at you?"

"Oh, that's not nice!"

She laughed. "I know, but I was a little worried about you; you weren't your usual charming self around her."

"And you still abandoned me to my fate!"

"I got my butt out of there. I hoped you'd do better without me around."

He smiled. "I did. I got over my initial awkwardness very quickly when you left."

"I'm glad to hear it. Are you going to see her again?"

A big smile spread across his face. "Yes, we're going out for dinner tomorrow."

"I'm so pleased for you." And she was. She felt terrible at the little pang of sadness she felt. How selfish was she that Toby having a girlfriend would make her sad? They spent most of their free time together and had done for years. She knew a lot of people, but she rarely hung out with anyone other than him.

If he and Sirena started dating, she'd no doubt see much less of him.

"Thanks, me too. You know how long I've liked her."

Hope nodded and gave him her best smile. "I do. I think it's awesome that you finally plucked up the courage."

"I think you're awesome that you helped me do it. You're the best, Hope." He raised his glass to her, but his smile seemed tinged with sadness.

"What's the matter? And don't say nothing. I know you too well."

"Okay. I suppose I just feel a little guilty."

Oh, no! Had he read her thoughts somehow? "Why?"

"Because I know you're still down in the dumps over Chance, and I'm asking you to celebrate with me."

She patted his hand. "I'm fine. You can't let me mar your happiness. And besides, I think I'm going to do what you said and make a big gesture."

"You are? What are you going to do?"

She smiled and shrugged. "I'm not sure yet." That wasn't entirely true. If she decided to be brave, she knew exactly what she was going to do. She knew Chance would either love it or hate it. What she didn't know yet was whether she was going to do it—or whether her words had just been a show of bravado to distract Toby from the fact that she was still wallowing in self-pity while he was finally getting to go out with Sirena.

"You know people were talking about you and Matt McLellan after you left the party?"

She sighed. "I thought they would be. That's why I got out of there so early. I needed to talk to him, but we were getting a lot of attention in just the five minutes we were standing there."

"I know. The gossip's already flying." He raised an eyebrow. "There's nothing to it, is there?"

"What do you think? Do you think I'd just forget Chance at the drop of a hat like that?"

"I don't think so, no, but people are saying maybe at the drop of a cowboy hat. They all saw the pictures of you and Chance. The next guy you're seen out with is a country singer. I'm just concerned. I don't think you need any more media attention."

"I know. That's why I left. That's the last thing I need. I did want to talk to him though, so I've invited him over here for lunch tomorrow. I thought that would be safer than being seen together out in public."

"What do you need to talk to him about?"

"Chance. Apparently, they're friends. Matt had seen the pictures of us and came to talk to me because he knows Chance and wanted to know if he's okay."

Toby shook his head. "If they're friends, why can't Matt check up on him himself?"

She shrugged. "They're not close friends."

"Evidently."

"What? Why have you gone all disapproving on me?"

"Because I don't understand why you would invite him over here, with the risk that carries, when it doesn't sound like he can tell you anything about Chance. And if you really wanted to know so badly, you could simply pick up the phone and call the guy."

Hope hung her head. "I know. But I don't want to blow it. I may only get one opportunity to speak to him ever again, and I want to go into that prepared."

Toby shook his head. "I'm no expert on these matters, as you know, but it feels wrong to me. I'm sure if you called Chance he'd talk to you. He'd explain why he left and either be willing to see you again or not."

"I know. You're right, but I suppose I'm trying to delay getting to the point where I find out that he doesn't want to see me again. Until that moment comes, then there's still a chance."

Toby smiled. "And a hope."

"Yeah."

~ ~ ~

Chance crammed his hat on his head and hurried out the door. The sun was already up, and he was running late. He couldn't remember the last time he'd gotten a late start. He couldn't help smiling—this one was thanks to Shane. Not because they'd stayed up late last night drinking beer; no, that'd happened hundreds of times. It was because his talk with Shane last night had finally set his mind at ease. He'd had his first good night's sleep in a month. He hurried up the path to the barn, swigging his coffee as he went.

He'd decided he was going to call Dr. Johnny tonight. Once he got done with the cattle, he'd make the call and ask for Hope's number. Then he was going to get straight on and call her. He wasn't going to put it off. Wasn't going to waste any time thinking about what he was going to say, how he was going to explain and apologize. And he sure as hell wasn't going to put himself through hell, waiting and wondering if she'd even want to talk to him anymore—or if she'd already forgotten him or found someone else. No. He wasn't going to put himself through any of that torture. As soon as he got done with work, he was going to do it. Bite the bullet, and just maybe they could start making up for lost time.

When he reached the barn, he headed for Maverick's stall first. Maverick was his buddy. He loved all the horses and rode most of them during the course of his work, but Maverick was special. Right now, he was lame. He came to the door and hung his head over when he heard Chance approach.

"Hey, buddy. How you feeling?" Chance rubbed his nose, and Maverick butted his shoulder. "I know, I'm sorry. I've missed you, too."

Maverick nodded his head, making Chance laugh.

"You get yourself all healed up, and we'll be back out again soon." He scratched the horse's ears and stroked his neck.

"Hello, Uncle Chancey!" A blur of pink topped with blonde curls came hurtling down the aisle between the stalls.

"Ruby. What are you up to?"

"Mommy said I could come and see Gypsy before I have to go to school."

Her mom appeared in the doorway. "How many times do I have to tell you not to run in the barn? Oh, hi Chance. Good morning."

"Morning, Corinne."

"Are you going for a ride? Can I come?" asked Ruby.

Corinne gave him an apologetic look as she approached and took hold of Ruby's hand. "No, sweetie. You know you can't. This is just a quick visit to Gypsy before we have to go. Chance is busy, and you have to go to school."

Chance tried to hide a smile as Ruby's bottom lip slid out. "But I …" He touched the tip of her nose with his thumb, making her stop and smile up at him. "What did you do that for?"

"Do what?" Chance shrugged at her innocently.

Her eyebrows knit together and she gave him a stern look. "I want to go out riding …"

Chance touched her nose again, making her giggle this time. "What are you doing? Why are you doing that to me?"

Chance smiled at Corinne who knew that what he was trying to do was avert a tantrum. "I don't know what you mean, but if you're supposed to see Gypsy before you go to school, hadn't you better hurry up?"

Ruby nodded and skipped away toward Gypsy's stall.

Corinne smiled at him. "Good tactic. It worked, thank you."

"I had to do something. I didn't want me being here to mess up your morning for you."

"Thanks, she loves seeing you. It's just that whenever she does, she wants to hang out with you and go riding."

"She's a sweetheart, but neither you nor I have time for it this morning. I need to get going."

Corinne nodded. "Are you taking Maverick out? I thought he was lame."

"He is. I just came to say hi to him."

Corinne smiled. "The horses really are your friends, aren't they?"

"Yeah." He couldn't help remembering riding out with Hope. She, too, had commented about the horses being his buddies. He shrugged. "I spend more time with them than with people. They're my coworkers, my team."

"I can see that. I love it. I love that Ruby gets to see it and learn from you, too."

"Thanks." Chance tipped his hat and made his way to Rio's stall. He'd been riding the tall, gray gelding for the last couple of weeks. He reminded Chance of Hercules, the horse he'd ridden in Oregon. He'd had the urge a couple of times now to call the stables out there and ask about Hercules. That was dumb though. He shook his head and started getting Rio ready for a day on the range. He didn't need to try salvaging memories of his time in Oregon. He could do better than that; tonight, he was going to call Hope.

When he was ready, he led Rio outside before he mounted up. He smiled as he watched Corinne's car pull away and waved back when he spotted Ruby's little hand waving madly at him. As he watched them disappear up the driveway he had to wonder what that kind of life might be like. Beau had been by himself until a year ago. He was a confirmed bachelor; no one thought he was likely to get married, but now he had Corinne and Ruby. He'd gone from spending his life alone, and being misunderstood, if not miserable, to being a happy family man with a full life. It was a huge change, but Beau was proof that it was possible.

He reined Rio around and set out toward the bottom pasture. He didn't need to pursue that line of thought just yet. He had a full day's work ahead of him, and even after that, he had a couple of phone calls to make before he'd find out if Hope even wanted to talk to him again.

~ ~ ~

Hope paced the living room as twelve-thirty approached. She was nervous—wasn't that silly? She'd invited Matt to come over for lunch, but she didn't even really know why. Well, in a general sense, she knew why; he was a connection to Chance. But it seemed it was a tenuous connection at best. As Toby had pointed out, if he and Chance were really friends, why had Matt come to ask her how he was? She shrugged. Tenuous or not, right now he was the only connection she had and silly as it might be, she didn't want to let it go. It was more than silly. It was risky. If rumors were flying about the two of them possibly being an item, then there was always the possibility of the press picking up on it. She really didn't need that.

She looked up when the intercom sounded. He was at the gate. She went to buzz him in and then waited at the front door while he parked his car. When he got out, he trotted up the steps with a big grin on his face. Removing his hat when he reached her, he held out his hand.

"Hello, again. Thanks for inviting me over."

She smiled. "Thanks for coming. Come on in."

Matt cast a wary glance back over his shoulder. "Yeah, we probably shouldn't stay on display out here too long, huh?"

Hope sighed and hurried him in.

"Do you think people know you're here?" she asked as she closed the door behind him.

"Probably. I've never known anything like this town. The press seems to know what you're doing before you know it yourself."

"They do." Hope was regretting asking him to come. The cost of the press making up a story about them seemed to outweigh any possible benefit of whatever he might be able to tell her about Chance.

"I'm sorry."

She pulled herself together and smiled. "It's not your fault. It goes with the territory. Come on through. Can I get you a drink?"

"Please. Something cold. Whatever you've got."

Hope led him through to the kitchen and gestured for him to take a seat at the island. She poured them each a lemonade, wondering as she did if his vagueness had been in the hopes of getting something alcoholic. She placed the glass in front of him. "Or would you prefer a beer?"

"No, this is great, thanks."

"What did you want to know about Chance?" It was hardly a polite way to open the conversation, but Hope didn't feel she needed to stand on ceremony.

Matt looked a little taken aback. "Honestly?"

She nodded.

"I don't really know. If you want the honest truth, I was feeling totally out of place at that party the other night. When I saw you, I figured you must be my kind of people, given that you and Chance were together." He shrugged and gave her a charming smile that she'd guessed worked wonders for him with the ladies. "I went for the only connection I had."

Hope sighed. She could hardly blame him for that, could she? She'd done the same thing.

"Sorry." Matt looked apologetic now.

She smiled. "That's okay. I'm doing the same thing right now. I invited you over to tell me whatever you could about him. How he's doing, what he's up to. But it seems we both know him, but neither of us knows him that well."

Matt nodded. "Yeah. I know he's a great guy. I can tell you that without hesitation."

"I know that much."

"Isn't it funny how a guy like that, a badass, a man of few words, can prove to both of us without ever even trying, that's he's one of the most decent human beings either of us has ever known?"

She gave a little laugh. "It is. I'd just like to see him again."

Matt raised an eyebrow. "Tell me it's none of my business if you want. Was the media attention too much for him? Is that why you're not together?"

"No." She hesitated. "At least, I don't think so."

Matt looked puzzled.

How could she explain to him—and why would she want to explain to him, stranger that he was?

"Like I said, it's none of my business, and I know it."

She smiled. "I just feel so stupid. He dumped me, and now I'm going around harassing his friends."

Matt laughed. "I don't think that's the case."

Hope laughed with him. "But you don't know, do you? I could be. The trouble is, even I don't know."

"Can I ask why? What happened between the two of you, I mean. Why did you break up?"

Hope shrugged. "I'd tell you if I knew, but I don't. He left without telling me. Perhaps I really am a crazy stalker lady who can't take the hint. Perhaps it's as simple as that, but I don't think so. I think if it were just a case of not wanting to see me anymore, he would have told me, made it clear, you know? I feel as though he thinks he's doing me a favor somehow by not being in my life."

Matt nodded. "And you haven't asked him?"

"No." Hope rolled her eyes. "I'm sounding crazier by the minute, right? At first, I was too upset. Then I hoped that he would change his mind. Then I decided I had to respect his decision. Then I started thinking maybe I should just call him and put myself out of my misery. And then ..."

"Then what?"

"Then I met you at Sirena's party and decided to wait until I'd spoken to you, to see if you could shed any light on things."

Matt smirked.

"What?" Her heart was racing thinking maybe he knew something she didn't. "Are you laughing at me? Am I being stupid? Is there some man-code you've spotted, and I don't know about, that means he dumped me and never wants to see me again?"

Matt chuckled. "Okay, now you are starting to sound a little crazy. Slow down. I was smiling because I was thinking that he's probably going through all the same things you are. I was smiling because when it comes to love, we can all be pretty dumb, no matter how smart we are."

Hope nodded sadly. "But what do you think?" She couldn't help asking.

He met her gaze and nodded solemnly. "You really want to know?"

She nodded eagerly.

"I think you should call the guy. I think that's the quickest, easiest way to put yourself out of your misery. Pick up the phone and call him. He'll either want to talk to you, or he won't. Either way, you'll know."

Hope nodded and gave him a rueful smile. "Thanks. Sorry I got you to come over here to tell me what common sense should have told me in the first place."

"That's okay. I get a free lunch and a new friend out of the deal."

She smiled and turned to the fridge for the sandwiches she'd prepared earlier. "You do, and if you want to eat outside, you get to enjoy one of the best views in town, too."

Chapter Six

Chance rode back into the yard and slid down from Rio. It had been a long, hard day. Much longer than he'd expected. He'd found a stretch of broken fence and had to round up three cows who'd managed to get out and roam onto the neighboring property. That particular stretch, where they'd breached the fence, adjoined the Davenport land. Between them, Johnny and Seymour must own several thousand acres. To think their houses were way back up the valley, near town, and yet the southernmost reaches of their land were all the way down here. Of course, it wasn't really their property that was on his mind. It was Hope. As soon as he'd taken care of Rio and put him away for the night, Chance was going to take a shower and call Johnny; then he was going to call Hope.

He untacked Rio and brushed him down, then led him through the barn to turn him out in the little pasture at the back.

"Evening." Mason was leaning against Storm's stall.

"What's up?"

Mason shook his head. The gesture seemed to say nothing was up, but the look on his face said something was. Chance walked on by leading Rio out through the gate at the back and closing it behind him before he returned. If something was up, Mason would no doubt tell him when he got there. "It's been a long day, and I want a shower and a beer. If you've got something to say, say it now, or come back to the cabin with me."

Mason nodded and fell into step beside him. *Shit.* That meant it was bad news, Chance just knew it.

"Okay. What is it?" asked Chance, as they started up the path to the cabin and Mason still hadn't spoken.

"I don't know yet, and it might be nothing. I've got Summer checking it out."

Chance stopped walking and turned to face him. "I don't do riddles. What the fuck are you talking about?"

Mason sighed. "Little Ruby saw Matt McLellan on TV today."

"And?" Chance had no idea what that could have to do with him.

"She remembered him from the weddings. He was here with Summer's sister, remember?"

"Yeah, he works with her. I think the two of them were together or wanted to be."

"We all thought that, but he was on TV today because they're saying he's got a new girlfriend."

Chance shook his head. "Why would I care? I mean, I like the guy. He helped us out big time with getting Guy Preston locked up, but why do you need to walk me home to tell me that he's got a new … Oh." It hit him. There was only one reason. He met Mason's gaze. "Hope?"

Mason nodded. "But you of all people know how wrong the press can get things."

Chance nodded. He did. Still, he felt like he'd had all the air knocked out of him. Just when he'd been planning to call her. When he'd finally gotten over his stupidity. It was too late. He'd missed his chance.

They got to the cabin and went inside. "What are you going to do?" asked Mason.

He shrugged. "Not a lot I can do, is there?"

"Coward!" They both spun around to see Shane sitting in the armchair, arms folded across his chest.

Chance glowered at him, but Shane got to his feet. Normally, he was like a big puppy—at six feet four, make that a very big puppy—but right now he seemed intimidating, even to Chance as he towered over him and glared down at him. "Yes, I let myself in. Yes, I'm calling you a coward again. I came here to make damned sure you call her tonight, just like you said you were going to. Nothing has changed since we talked. Well, the only thing you know for sure is that the press has run a story on her. So, you call her, and you ask her yourself. Okay?"

Chance stared up at him for a long moment. He was wrestling with sadness that Hope had moved on, with anger that Shane dared to try to intimidate him like that, and with gratitude that both Mason and Shane cared enough to be here right now. Eventually, he laughed. "Okay! Yes sir, Shane, sir. Would you mind if I have a shower first, though?"

Shane stepped back looking a little stunned. "Sure. You're not going to yell at me? Or argue with me or anything?"

Chance shook his head. "Nah. I don't see the point. You're right. I can't let this knock me off track, can I?"

"No," said Mason. "You can't." He grinned at Shane. "Thanks, little brother, you made this a damned sight easier than I thought it was going to be."

Chance laughed. "You have no idea. Little brother here gave me a good talking to last night and set me straight about a few things."

Shane grinned. "I wasn't sure if any of it had stuck and when I heard about the story on Hope and Matt, I had to come check on you. I can't see there being anything between them. Matt seemed pretty stuck on Summer's sister, but you need to call her and talk to her yourself. You can't use this as another excuse."

Chance nodded. "I agree."

Mason and Shane exchanged a glance before Mason turned back to Chance. "Do you want us to stick around?"

"No." Chance smirked at him. "Like I told you the other day, we're not a bunch of girlies. I've got this." He sucked in a deep breath then blew it out slowly before adding, "Seriously. I'm not going to chicken out. I just want to take that shower and gather my thoughts. I need to do this by myself."

Mason nodded. "Okay." He started herding Shane toward the door.

Shane stopped and looked back. "You going to call me later?"

Chance chuckled. "Maybe."

Once they'd gone, his smile faded. Would he want to call Shane later? How would he feel if he talked to Hope and she was with Matt—if she'd moved on so quickly and easily? He headed for the shower. He couldn't waste time wondering. He needed to just get on and do it. Half an hour later, he was dried and dressed and sitting on the back porch with his phone in one hand and a beer in the other. The first call would be the easier of the two, but he still wasn't looking forward to making it. He took a swig of his beer, then hit the button and waited while it rang.

"Hello?"

"Dr. Johnny. Hi, it's Chance Malone."

"Oh, hello Chance, what can I do for you?" Johnny sounded distracted.

"I ... err ... I wondered..." *Jeez!* He needed to get a grip. "Could you give me Hope's number?"

"Of course. Do you have a pen?"

"I do." Chance picked up the pad and pen he'd brought out with him, though he had a feeling that once he heard her number, he wouldn't forget it in a hurry. He jotted down the numbers as Johnny said them, remembering as he did the first time he'd written his own number down for Hope. "Thanks."

"You're welcome. Is there anything else?"

"No, sir, that was all, thank you."

"Okay, goodbye."

Chance was surprised to hear the line go dead. He'd expected at least some questions over why he wanted Hope's number, and why he didn't have it. He shook his head. Oh well, he had what he wanted. Now it was time to make the call that mattered.

He didn't allow himself to hesitate, knowing that if he did, he could waste all kinds of time wondering what he should say, and what she might say. He tapped in the number and listened to it ring.

"You've reached Hope Davenport. I'll be unavailable for the next few days. Please contact Davenport Athleticwear with any urgent matters."

Chance hit the end call button and blew out a sigh. Even though he hadn't spent any time building up to it, his heart was racing in his chest. He'd been prepared for one of the most important calls of his life. Reaching the message had been anti-climactic, to say the least. There wasn't even a way to leave her a voicemail. He sure as hell wasn't going to call her office and try to run her down that way. What was he going to do? He could call Johnny back and ask if he knew what was going on. He took another swig of his beer. No. He shouldn't do that. Asking for her number had been one thing, but involving her uncle was another. He shrugged and stared out at the mountains. He'd wait a couple of days and try again. In the meantime, he'd just have to try not to drive himself crazy wondering if she was hiding from the press because of Matt— or with Matt.

~ ~ ~

Hope looked around her as she made her way down the steps from the jet. The sky was as big and blue as she remembered it. The mountains were much greener, though still topped with snow. Montana still felt like home. She got on the golf cart that was waiting to take her to the general aviation building. She was fairly certain there would be no press waiting for her here.

When the doors slid open and she stepped inside she was relieved to see that she was right. There were two girls sitting at the reception desk. A couple was sitting on the big sofas by the window, watching a commercial jet coming in to land. A pilot stood by the coffee machine, but that was all. She let out a sigh of relief.

"There you are!"

She smiled when she saw Aunt Jean hurrying toward her with Uncle Johnny in her wake. "It's so good to see you," she said as her aunt wrapped her in a hug.

"It's even better to see you, dear. I'm sorry the press is hounding you again, but I can't say I'm sorry it's brought you up here to visit. It's been far too long."

Hope nodded and turned to Uncle Johnny. "Thanks for coming to get me."

He nodded. "Of course." She sensed there was something not right with him, but he smiled brightly. "Let's get you home then. You're coming for dinner with us this evening."

"Thanks." Aunt Jean had invited her to stay with them, but she'd declined, preferring instead to stay at Oscar's place. She didn't want to be any trouble, but she also wanted to be by herself. Who was she kidding? What she really wanted was to see Chance, and to be able to invite him over to see her. She wouldn't be able to do that if she stayed with her aunt and uncle.

It was a forty-minute drive from the Bozeman airport to their house in Paradise Valley, just south of Livingston. Hope smiled as they drove up the tree-lined driveway to the house. Their house held so many happy memories for her. Memories of her childhood and her cousins. She drew in a deep breath—memories of her mom.

"Come on inside," said Aunt Jean when they pulled up. "Brody will take your bags over to Oscar's place for you."

Hope smiled. Brody had managed the place for them ever since she could remember. She felt a little guilty, though, having him take care of her bags. Last time she'd been here, she'd been shocked by how old he seemed.

As her aunt led her up the steps to the front door, she was puzzled by the sight of a man in his thirties, a very good-looking man in butt hugging Wranglers, getting into the car.

Uncle Johnny laughed. "That's Brody Junior. You probably don't recognize him."

"Oh!" she certainly hadn't recognized him. Her memory of Brody Jr. was a shy kid who hung around the horses and would watch her and her cousins play, but never joined in.

Aunt Jean smiled. "Don't look so shocked; you're not the only one who went and grew up on us."

Hope nodded. Of course, she wasn't.

She enjoyed dinner with her aunt and uncle. She always enjoyed any time she got to spend with them. Nonetheless, she was glad when it was over. She couldn't wait to excuse herself and be allowed to go down to Oscar's house and get settled in. She'd called him after the story about her and Matt had hit the news. It was crazy; they were all over the papers and TV. There was all kinds of speculation about the two of them. When the crowds of reporters had gathered outside her front gate for the second time in less than two months, she'd decided it was time to leave town again. She'd considered going back to Oregon, but there was no point. She'd only be going there to feel close to Chance again, and he wasn't there. He was here. She didn't know if he'd want to see her—especially if he'd seen the stories about her and Matt—but at least she'd be in the same valley as him. She'd be here when she made her grand gesture. And if he wanted to see her, she'd be just a few miles up the road.

"Shall I take you down to Oscar's?" asked Uncle Johnny. "You look tired."

She smiled gratefully. "That'd be wonderful, thank you. I'll come see you tomorrow, Aunt Jean."

"You come if you want to, don't if you don't. You're here for a break. You know how things work around here. We don't stand on ceremony, and there are no expectations. If you want some company, come up and say hello. If you want your peace and quiet, you hang out down there by the river and enjoy your own company."

Hope hugged her tight. "Thanks."

"Of course. Goodnight, dear."

"Do you want to drive down or walk?" asked Uncle Johnny when they got outside.

"I'd love to walk if you don't mind walking back up."

Johnny chuckled. "You know me better than that. You're my excuse to get out for a stroll on a perfect evening."

Hope slipped her arm through his, and they set out down the lane that led to Oscar's place.

They walked in silence for a while. Enjoying the peace and quiet, the only sounds were the rushing of the river and birdsong. Hope could feel herself beginning to relax as they went.

"Are you okay?" asked Uncle Johnny after a while.

She nodded. "I am. I just didn't need to be at the center of another media circus."

"I know. And what about Chance?"

She met his gaze. "What about him?"

"Isn't he why you're here?"

"No! Well, partly. Okay. Yes. But I don't even know if he wants to talk to me, let alone see me."

"Damn!"

She was shocked, Uncle Johnny rarely ever cursed. "What? What's wrong?"

"I'm sorry Hope. It completely slipped my mind. He called me, last night."

"Chance did?"

"Yes. Asking for your number. I'd swear I'm starting to lose my mind. I was busy when he called. I was going to call you and tell you, but then Jean called me outside, and I forgot."

"When you called this morning, I assumed that the two of you must have spoken and that was why you wanted to come."

Hope shook her head. Her mind was racing. "He hasn't called me. Did he say what he wanted?"

"Just your number."

Hope frowned, wondering why he hadn't called. It was her turn to curse. "Damn! He may have called, but he wouldn't have got through. I switched my phone off and left an I'm-unavailable-call-the-office-if-you-need-me message on it."

Uncle Johnny smiled. "Then perhaps you'd better call him?"

Hope thought about it as they approached the house. "I will."

"Good. Whatever went wrong between the two of you, I'd like to see you put it right."

"Thanks, Uncle Johnny, I would too. I just wish ..."

"Don't worry about your father. I'll help you with him if it's necessary."

Hope flung her arms around his neck and hugged him tightly. "Thanks, Uncle Johnny. You're the best!"

He laughed. "I have my uses; I'll admit that much. But remember Hope, your father cares; he just isn't very good at showing it. He wants to protect you, and he wants you to maintain your independence, at the same time. That's not an easy line to walk—not for anyone—but especially not for your father."

Hope sighed. "I know. I just wish he'd try listening to me, sometimes. You know, being close instead of being in charge?"

"I do know, but he was never very good at being close to anyone. He was close to your mom, but after … after she was gone, he never dared open his heart again."

"I know. But I wish he hadn't closed me out when he closed the rest of the world out. I lost her, too. She was my mom. I was twelve years old." She stopped. She wasn't going to go getting all emotional; Uncle Johnny shouldn't have to deal with that.

He wrapped his arm around her shoulders. "I understand, sweetheart. He did the best he could. He still does."

Hope nodded. She knew it was true. How could she ask for more from her father than he was capable of giving? Even if she needed more from him.

When Uncle Johnny left, she unpacked her things and wandered around the house looking out the windows at the mountains and the river rushing by below the deck. She loved this place, but that wasn't why she was staring out the windows. No, she was trying to pluck up the courage to call Chance. She was thrilled that he'd asked Uncle Johnny for her number, she hoped it meant that there was a chance for them, but she wasn't totally sure. She blew out a big sigh. She wasn't sure? Well then, all she could do was call him and find out.

Chapter Seven

Chance sat on the back porch with his hands folded behind his head and his feet up on the table. He felt like shit. He'd had this weird gnawing feeling inside him all day. He needed to talk to Hope. He needed to know if she was seeing Matt. And if she wasn't, he needed to know if she wanted to see him again. He'd been turning it over and over in his mind all day. Even if the story about her and Matt was just the press making something out of nothing, that didn't necessarily mean that she'd want to see him. She might hate him for having walked out on her; even though logic told him that wasn't the case. Dr. Johnny would surely have treated him differently if it was the case. Granted, he had been short with Chance on the phone, but he'd still given him Hope's number. Another possibility was that she wasn't mad at him at all, she might just be indifferent. She might have been fine with him walking away at the end of their stay in Oregon. That had been the original plan; in fact, that had been what she suggested. Maybe she was fine with it all, and he was blowing everything out of proportion? He took his feet down from the table and leaned forward, resting his head in his hands. He was blowing it all out of proportion, that was for sure. This wasn't him; this wasn't what he did. He didn't waste his time sitting around driving himself nuts over ifs, buts, and maybes. And certainly not over a woman. He looked up at the perfect blue sky. What would Chloe think if she could see him now? They used to laugh together at the drama other couples created. They'd each helped their friends through teenage heartbreak and witnessed the angst caused by misunderstandings and false starts. He sighed. Chloe would kick his ass for him right now, he was sure of it. But what would she tell him to do? He was being pathetic, but only because he didn't know what he could do. If he could call Hope, he would. He looked at his phone sitting on the table and jumped like a startled rabbit when it began to ring. He made a face; it was no doubt Mason or Shane checking up on him.

He picked it up and stared at the screen. The name on the display was Hope. He stared at it a moment longer trying to process. Then he gave himself a shake and hit the answer button.

"Hope?"

"Chance!"

A big grin spread across his face at the sound of her voice. "Hey."

"Hi."

"How are you?"

She laughed. "Grateful that you can't see me right now. I'm grinning like an idiot and hopping around. I didn't know if you'd answer."

He chuckled. "I wish I could see you right now. You'd laugh at me, too, I'm doing about the same thing you are."

"You are?"

"Sure am."

"Yay! So, you're pleased to hear from me?"

"Happier than you know. I tried to call you."

"Uncle Johnny told me you'd asked for my number. I'm sorry there was no way to leave a message."

"I was too, but it doesn't matter now, does it?"

"It doesn't. It's so good to hear your voice. I've missed you."
Chance felt his throat tighten and had to blink a couple of times. "I've missed you too, honey." She made a strangled little sound that made his heart clench. "Are you okay?"

"Yes! I'm sorry." He could hear the tears in her voice. "I ... I ... Oh, screw it! I'm going to say it; you can no doubt hear it. I'm blubbing here."

He smiled. "I thought I just got something in my eye."

"You mean, you ...?"

"Yeah." He wasn't going to say it out loud, or he might just really start to blub. "I'm sorry, you know. I screwed up, the way I left."

"It's okay. You did what you needed to do. I'm not going to say I understand, but I respect your choice."

Chance closed his eyes. That was what he loved about her. No drama, no demanding explanations. "Thank you. It was the wrong choice."

"It was?"

"It was for me. It might have been the best choice for you."

"No, it was the wrong one for me too, but you made it, all I could do was respect it."

Chance nodded. "Is there any way you'd give me a second chance?"

She laughed. "I'm the one who's hoping for a second chance."

"If you still want this one, you've got him. He's all yours."

He could hear the smile in her voice. "I like the sound of that. When?"

"I don't know. I'll come out there, I'll find a way."

"Oh, shit!"

"What?" Chance frowned.

"I'm an idiot. You don't know I'm here."

He frowned harder. "What do you mean?"

"I mean, I'm right here. In Paradise Valley."

"You are?" His heart began to pound in his chest. "You're at your Uncle's?"

"Yes! There was another stupid story in the press about me and ... did you see it?"

"I did." It didn't matter anymore. He already knew it wasn't true.

"Chance, there's no truth ..."

"It's okay. I understand."

"No. You don't. You have to listen, hear me out. The only reason I ever even talked to Matt was about you. I ran into him at a party, and he said he knew you. I couldn't talk to him there because people were watching us. I stupidly invited him over for lunch, thinking that would be away from the gossipmongers and hoping he'd be able to tell me how you were, and if ... if ..."

Chance was smiling now. Her explanation made him happier than he would have believed possible. "If what."

"Oh, you! You're going to make me say it, aren't you?"

"You're the one who told me I had to listen. So, yeah, go on. You were hoping he could tell you if ..."

She laughed. "I'll get you back for this. If he thought I still stood a chance."

Chance closed his eyes and smiled.

"Say something."

"You do. You have a Chance. Do I have a Hope?"

Her voice sounded so tender as she replied, "You do."

"Can I come see you?"

"Yes, please, or shall I come to you?"

"You don't know where I am."

"I don't care. I'll find you."

He chuckled. "It'll take me twenty minutes to get to you."

"Do I have to wait that long? Can I meet you halfway? Say, at the Mill Creek turnoff?"

"Only if you're sure you have a reliable vehicle and you know exactly where you're going."

She laughed. "Have a little faith in me?"

"I do."

"Okay, then I'm going to hang up on you now, and I'll see you in ten minutes."

~ ~ ~

Hope grabbed the keys to Oscar's Land Rover from the bowl on the entry table, grateful that he'd told her where they'd be. As she drove up by her aunt and uncle's house, she pulled her phone out, not wanting them to worry.

Uncle Johnny answered. "Do I need to guess where you're going?"

"I think you know."

"I think I do. Have a good time. Thanks for calling."

"I didn't want you to worry."

"Thanks. Let me know if you won't be back tonight. Just text."

She felt the heat in her cheeks. She was a grown woman, but back here she was still little Hopey, and Uncle Johnny was looking out for her.

"I will."

She checked herself in the rearview mirror before she turned out onto East River Road. She would have retouched her makeup if she'd had more time, but it didn't matter. What mattered was getting to Chance, just as fast as she could.

When she approached the turnout, he was already there. She knew it was him. A big black pickup sat in the parking lot. It had to be Chance's vehicle. It was big and strong and obviously no stranger to hard work. She pulled in beside it and peered into the cab. There he was, smiling back at her. Her heart leaped, and her hands began to shake.

She opened the door and ran around to meet him. He climbed out of the truck and hurried toward her, then stopped a few feet away. She stopped, too, and met his gaze. Those beautiful light blue eyes were shining. "Hope."

She loved the sound of her name on his lips. She smiled and nodded, not sure she'd be able to speak around the lump in her throat. He held his arms wide open, and she flung herself at him. Those big strong arms closed around her and crushed her to his chest. He felt like home. She buried her face in his chest and breathed him in. "I missed you so much."

He tucked his fingers under her chin and tilted her head up. The pain in his eyes took her breath away. "I'm so sorry."

She shook her head rapidly. "It doesn't matter. What matters is that we're here now. Together." She slid her arms up around his neck.

He nodded and closed his arms tight around her waist pulling her against him as he lowered his lips to hers. She closed her eyes, and a shiver ran down her spine as he nipped her bottom lip. Then his mouth claimed hers in a way he hadn't done before—it was a demanding kiss, his tongue sweeping inside her mouth, his arms crushing her to him. She clung to him as she kissed him back, needing him for support as her knees went weak and never wanting to let go of him again. That kiss felt like both an awakening and a homecoming. In it, her body remembered every kiss, every touch they'd shared, and her whole being felt a sense of belonging, of peace at being back in the place she belonged.

It was a long time before their lips finally parted and he lifted his head. He looked dazed—she felt dazed. They stared into each other eyes until he eventually nodded, as though some decision had been made, some question answered. Part of her felt that she knew the question and the answer. Was this it? Was it right? Were they meant to be? In that kiss, the answer had been given, and it was a resounding *yes*.

There was so much to be said, but words weren't going to do it. He unwrapped his arms from her waist and took hold of her hand. "Do you want to stay with me?"

She nodded. She did, in whatever sense he meant it.

He led her to his truck, then hesitated, looking at the Land Rover. "Should we take that thing home first? I'd hate to leave it sitting out here by itself."

Hope sighed. If it were her vehicle, she wouldn't care, but it wasn't. She could drive it back to Oscar's place, and Chance could follow her up there, but she wanted to go to Chance's place, to be in his home. That was important to her somehow. "I could follow you in it?"

Chance pressed his lips together.

She smiled. "What's up, are you worried about the neighbors seeing a strange car outside your house?"

He gave her a wry smile. "It's not about neighbors, remember I told you, I live on the ranch. Every single Remington will have seen or heard about that Land Rover by morning, and they'll all know what it means."

"They will?"

He shrugged and looked the tiniest bit embarrassed. "They've been worried about me since I came back."

Her smile grew wider. "They know about me?"

"Yeah, I'm sorry, I …"

She laughed. "I'm not sorry, I'm thrilled."

He stepped closer, trapping her between his body and his truck. "I'm glad."

Her arms came up around his neck again, and soon she was lost in another kiss. She wanted to melt into him, his body felt hot and hard, pressed against hers. She wished there were no clothes keeping his skin from touching hers. He lifted his head abruptly. "Wherever we're going, however we're getting there, we need to go now."

"Well, I don't care who sees me if you don't. The way I see it, either I can follow you home, or we can climb in the back of your truck."

He chuckled. "You'd better follow me then. The back of the truck can wait until a starry night in the summer."

As she climbed back into the Land Rover, Hope had to smile. She'd like to think they'd still be together when the summer rolled around—and beyond.

~ ~ ~

Chance pulled out onto the road and checked his rearview mirror; not so much to make sure Hope was following as to make sure she was there—that he wasn't imagining this. Half an hour ago he hadn't known if he'd ever see her again and yet here she was following him home. He grinned to himself and put his foot down.

When he turned into the driveway of Remington Ranch, his grin faded. Would he make it to the cabin without running into anyone? Mason and Gina might be around; they liked to take a stroll with baby Phoenix in the evenings. Shane might still be at the guest ranch. Beau and Corinne might be visiting the barn with little Ruby. He shrugged. What did it matter? It wasn't that he wanted to hide Hope from them. No, it wasn't that at all. It was just that he wanted her all to himself. He didn't want to waste precious time introducing her to the family. That would come, he hoped, but for tonight he wanted it to be about the two of them. He drove past the guest ranch and the barn without seeing anyone but the horses. He pulled up outside the cabin and a few moments later, Hope pulled up beside him and jumped out of the Land Rover.

"It's beautiful!"

He nodded. "It is, but right now all I can see is you."

"Aww, did someone give you lessons in sweet talking since I saw you last?" Chance narrowed his eyes at her, and she laughed. "What? I don't remember you talking like that before."

"I didn't know what a good thing I had then, did I? Now I've missed you for over a month, I need to tell you what I think when I think it."

She came to him and slid her arms around his waist, looking up into his eyes. "What, instead of leaving me a note about it and disappearing?"

He closed his eyes for a moment, regretting that as one of the dumbest decisions he'd ever made. "Yeah. Something like that." He drew her closer and dropped a kiss on her lips. "I'm sorry."

She smiled. "Don't be. It's over, done with. We learn from it and move on."

He nodded. He'd never been very good at that.

"Are you going to invite me in?"

"Yeah. Welcome to my humble abode." He took her by the hand and led her to the front door, wondering as he did how messy it was in there. He took pretty good care of the place, but he knew it wasn't anything like she was used to.

Once they were inside, she stopped and looked around. "Oh, Chance. I love it!"

He raised an eyebrow at her. "You do?"

She nodded enthusiastically. "It's perfect; it's real. Normally when you see a log cabin, it's nice, but it's fake. They're usually wannabes, but this is the real deal." She wandered around the living room taking everything in. "I love it. It's you."

He smiled. "Thanks." Now she was here, he wasn't sure what to do. Back up at Mill Creek, there had been an urgency between them, he'd needed to get her back into bed, to reconnect in every sense. He still felt that need, but the moment had been broken. He wasn't sure she still felt it. "Do you want a drink? I have some of that wine."

She stepped toward him. "I'd like some, but there's something else I'd like more first." She rested her hands on his waist and tugged on his belt, pulling him closer until his hips touched hers.

He looked down into her eyes; they were glazed with lust. Putting his hands on her shoulders, he smiled. Now he knew what to do. He brushed his lips over hers then took her by surprise by scooping her up into his arms, just like he had all those times in Oregon when her ankle was bad.

Her arms came up around his neck, and she smiled as he carried her into his bedroom.

"I missed you," she whispered as he set her down on the bed.

"I missed you more, honey. I was such a damned fool. I shouldn't ..."

She reached up and pressed a finger to his lips. "Please, don't. I want to be here in this moment. I want to enjoy you; I want you to enjoy me. Let's be happy and focus on now. Leave the past behind?"

He caught his breath, feeling for a moment as though her request was about so much more than regretting the way he'd walked out on her. Choosing to be with her meant choosing to leave the past behind, didn't it? He nodded slowly, as much to himself as to her. Even though part of him still wanted to cling to the past, to Chloe, he knew now that a bigger, better part of him wanted to be with Hope—happy and in the present.

He nodded and lay down beside her, drawing her close until her soft, warm body was pressed against his. She felt so right, so welcoming, so ... his.

Chapter Eight

Hope wrestled with the buckle on his jeans. She'd seen something change in his eyes when she'd asked him to leave the past behind. She'd only meant she wanted to forget the way they'd parted, but she knew that when he'd nodded, he was agreeing to something more than that.

His rough hands made short work of removing her clothes; she was naked before she'd even won the battle with his buckle.

He smiled. "Do you want a hand with that?"

She pursed her lips and cupped his erection through his jeans. "Only if you want a hand with that."

He chuckled and unfastened it himself, then shrugged out of his shirt. She licked her lips; she couldn't help it. The sight of his muscular chest and strong arms had her tugging at his jeans to get him out of them. Once he lay naked beside her, she knelt up, running her hands over his chest and on down. She traced the V that led south with her fingertip, loving the way he closed his eyes and let out a deep breath. She closed her hand around him and had to lick her lips again. He was so hot and hard, so ready for her, just as she was ready for him.

He opened his eyes as she straddled him and smiled as she began to stroke herself with him. She was already wet, and she stroked herself with the very tip of him, tormenting them both until she couldn't stand it any longer.

His hands came up and closed around her hips, lifting her to receive him. She met his gaze and positioned him at her entrance. Chance thrust up, and she impaled herself on him as they both moved and gasped together. She felt as though she was losing her grip on reality as she rode him, his hips bucking wildly underneath her, his hands holding her steady in place.

His gaze never left hers, his eyes boring into hers, telling her so much, asking so many questions. She rocked her hips in time with his, taking him ever deeper as the tension in her belly started to build. Whatever questions he was asking, her answers were all the same. As he took her closer to the edge, she realized she was answering him aloud. "Yes, yes, *yes!*" She screamed as her orgasm tore through her and she felt him tense. His grasp on her hips tightened, and he pulled her down to take him harder at the moment he found his release. "Yes!" He gasped as they soared away together.

Eventually, she slumped down onto his chest. His arms came up around her. One hand tangling in her hair. "I ... you, Hope."

She froze. Had he just said what she thought he had?

She lifted her head and looked down into his eyes.

"I missed you so much, honey."

She nodded. "I missed you." Was that what he'd said the first time, I miss you?

She rested her head back down on his shoulder and wondered as he continued to stroke her hair and tried to figure out whether she was relieved or disappointed that the word had been missed and not love.

~ ~ ~

Chance watched her sip her wine; she was so damned beautiful. He still couldn't quite believe she was really here.

But she was. She was sitting out here on his back porch with him, though right now he wanted to drag her back to bed— the way she looked in one of his shirts and nothing else had him struggling to concentrate on anything but thoughts of laying her down again.

She looked up at him with a smile. "This place is perfect. It's so you."

"It is?"

She nodded. "It's rugged and it's beautiful. It's harsh somehow, but only because it's strong, too strong to tolerate weakness."

"Do you think I'm harsh?"

She smiled. "Not in a bad way. You're real. There's a reason they call reality harsh. That's not a bad thing. It's a good thing, if you ask me."

"Thanks, I think." He smiled. She nodded and stared out at the mountains, sipping her wine. He couldn't believe the words that had come out of his mouth after they'd made love. The only woman he'd ever said those three words to was Chloe. He was glad Hope hadn't heard them or hadn't believed them, at least. Either way, she hadn't pushed him about them. Even if they were true, it'd take him a long time of figuring them out and being prepared to believe them himself before he said them to her again. He didn't even know what she was thinking. "How long are you here for?"

She turned and met his gaze. "I don't know. I think that will depend on you."

He tried to hide his smile but didn't quite manage it. "I thought you were just here to hide from the press?"

She laughed. "No, you didn't. You know damned well I could have hidden anywhere. I came here because of you."

He nodded. "I'm glad, but now I want to know how long I get to keep you? Is this for a couple of days, a couple of weeks?"

Or the rest of your life? Damn! He hoped to hell he hadn't said that last part out loud.

"You tell me. I can stay for days or weeks …" She looked more serious as she met his gaze. "Or months."

Wow. Chance nodded. "I guess we'll have to see how quickly I piss you off, then, huh?"

She chuckled. "Or how quickly you get bored with me again and want rid of me."

He shook his head and reached across the table for her hand. "You know damned well I didn't get bored of you."

"I do. I was only teasing."

"But you need to know why I left that way, right?"

She shrugged. "I won't lie. I'd like to know, but I can live with the fact that you had your reasons."

He squeezed her hand. "Thanks." He wanted to laugh at the disappointed look on her face. "It's okay; I am going to tell you."

"Phew! Thanks."

"Did you talk to your dad after I left?"

Hope nodded. "I did."

"And was he relieved that I was gone?"

Her eyebrows knit together. "Yes." She started to look angry. "He didn't get to you, did he? Did he talk to you, warn you away?"

Chance shook his head rapidly. "No, nothing like that at all. I was up in the night, for a drink of water. Your phone was going off like crazy, and I'm sorry, but I looked. I saw all those messages from your dad."

Hope sighed. "And you decided for me."

He nodded. "I know I shouldn't have, but if I had to make the decision again today, I'm not sure I'd be able to do any different."

"Why? I thought you were glad that we're past that. I thought you were happy to see me again?"

He squeezed her hand. "You know I am, but I'm still worried about what it might do to your dad, more importantly to your relationship with him."

Hope shrugged. "We don't have much of a relationship."

"But it's better than it used to be, right?"

She nodded. "It is, we've come a long way in the last few years."

"And that's what he said that made me leave. I told you my dad and I didn't talk for a long time, I know what it's like to be close to him again now, to regret the years we lost. I don't want to be responsible for destroying the progress you and your dad have made. Your relationship with him is more important."

"Is it?"

His heart raced in his chest both at the question and the look in her eyes as she asked it. "I thought so."

She nodded but didn't say anything.

No matter what she might mean about how important Chance was to her, he was curious about her relationship with her dad. "Do you want to tell me about it?"

"About what?"

He was surprised that for the first time she seemed evasive. He shrugged. "If you don't know, then I guess it doesn't matter."

She sighed. "Of course, I know what you mean, but I guess my reaction means, no, I don't want to talk about it." She met his gaze. "That's not because of you, though. It's because of me. I don't know how I feel about it, about him, other than it hurts. There's so much unresolved between us. He didn't want me to see you anymore, and that hurt me. It hurt me for so many reasons—he doesn't know you, he doesn't know me. The only thing that was important to him was his own take on the situation." She shrugged. "I did talk to him a little about it afterward, and he was more understanding, you could even say supportive, but then again …" she let her words trail off.

Chance nodded. "That might just have been because he thought I was out of the picture?"

Hope sighed. "Yeah. To him, it seems that once someone is out of the picture, there's no need to discuss it anymore."

"Are you talking about your mom?"

"I am. He was devastated when she died. I get that, but I was, too, and I was twelve years old." There were tears in her eyes. "He shut down; he did what he needed to do to survive. He removed himself from everything that reminded him of her and lost himself in his work. I understand why he did what he did, but understanding his needs doesn't help with the fact that he didn't understand mine—or do anything to meet them. I had to cope all by myself. He took me away from here, from Uncle Johnny and Aunt Jean and the boys. He wanted to isolate himself, but he isolated me, too."

Chance went to kneel beside her. "I'm sorry." He wiped a tear from under her eye with his thumb.

She shook her head and smiled at him. "No, I'm sorry. I don't usually whine about it."

"You're not whining. I asked you to tell me, and you are."

She shrugged. "Maybe, but I'm also feeling sorry for myself, and that won't get me anywhere."

He nodded. "Let me guess, that's what he used to tell you?"

Fresh tears spilled down her cheeks. "Yes, but that's his way of coping. He was trying to help me. He thought I could cope that way, too."

"But you were twelve, just a little girl."

"I know, but he did the best he could."

Chance nodded. "And he loves you, and you love him."

She nodded. "The best we can, yes."

"That's all anyone can ever do, isn't it?"

"Exactly, which is why it feels terrible to admit that I want more from him. Anyway," she smiled brightly at him, "I appreciate your reasons for leaving like you did, and I'm glad you told me, but in future, please would you talk to me and not make the decision for me?"

"I will. I thought I was doing what was best for you." As he said the words, Chance could see that what he'd done was the same as what her father had done. He'd decided what was best for her without considering what she wanted. "I'm sorry."

She stared down into her glass for a moment then looked up at him. "I'm sorry, too. I'm sorry that my glass is empty. I like to keep it at least half full. Is there any chance of a top up?"

He smiled, he got the message—conversation closed. He went inside and brought the bottle out. When he returned to the porch, his heart clenched in his chest. This felt so right. Having her here, seeing her beauty against the backdrop of the mountains. For a moment, he could imagine that this was his life—that she was his woman. It was only a fleeting moment, though. Having her here might seem like a wonderful life to him, but how would it seem to her? Her life was in LA where she had a business and friends and obligations. He remembered thinking that about her before when he'd talked about buying Hercules—it was easy to transplant a horse into a new life, it was a bit more difficult with humans.

She smiled up at him. "What are you thinking?"

He shook his head. How could he tell her?

"Before we got onto the subject of my dad, we were talking about how long I might stay."

Yeah, and he'd just been wondering whether it might extend to a lifetime. He couldn't tell her that. He'd need to be damned sure about how he felt first. He'd need to be sure he wasn't just swept up in the moment, the excitement, the happiness of being with her again. "And how long do you think that might be?"

She met his gaze, as if she knew what he was thinking, but wasn't prepared to talk about it yet, either. "Well, I told Toby not to expect me back for the next couple of weeks, at least."

Chance smiled, relieved that it wasn't just a couple of days. "So, are we looking at Hope and Chance, the second installment, another two-week interlude?"

"I guess so. What do you think?"

He nodded. "It gives you another opt-out clause, doesn't it?"

She laughed. "I'm not the one who wants it. I just know that I've landed myself into your life without any warning."

"You have, but I'm glad."

"Then I guess we just play it by ear again. That's all we can do. We can take this couple of weeks and see where things go. Treat it the same as we did in Oregon. We have an end date; we can extend it if we want to. And if we don't, we walk away as friends."

Chance came around the table and refilled her glass. "You've got yourself a deal." He wanted to say that he hoped their end date would never come, that he wanted her to be so much more than a friend, but he didn't dare. He didn't know for certain that he'd be able to do it, didn't know that she'd even want to, not when she got to know him, when she saw him in his life.

She held her glass out to him. "Then let's drink to it."

He touched his glass against hers.

"For now, at least, we have a Chance and a Hope," she said with a smile.

"What more could we ask for?"

~ ~ ~

Hope looked up into his eyes and nodded. She couldn't ask for anything more than a Chance. She knew that now. Being with him again, seeing him here in his life, his world, she just knew. She'd never felt like this about a guy before. She hadn't known him long, but she felt as though she knew him better than she'd ever known Drew. She felt as though Chance knew her, too. She'd never talked to Drew about her relationship with her dad. He'd never even asked her about her mom. "It'll be different here, though, won't it? Different than it was in Oregon."

"What do you mean?"

"Well, when we were there we were both on vacation, away from our everyday lives. I'm on vacation again here, but you're not. I mean, I'm guessing you'll have to go to work in the morning, and I'll have to go back to Oscar's place, and ..."

Chance's phone started to ring. "Sorry. I don't need to get that."

"It's okay. You should at least see who it is."

He pressed his lips together and reluctantly pulled it out of his back pocket.

"Take it," she said. She could tell by the look on his face that he needed to.

He sighed. "Sorry." He hit the button to answer the call. "What's up, Mason?"

She watched his face. He seemed half-amused, half-irritated.

"Yes." He rolled his eyes at her with a half-smile. "No, thank you. You don't need to do that ... Seriously ...? Okay. If you insist ... Yeah, all right. I'll see you." He hung up with a smile on his face.

Hope waited.

"That was Mason."

"He's the eldest brother, right? The one you're closest to?"

"Yeah, though we're all close. He and his wife Gina live up at the big house now." He pointed to the beautiful ranch house up on the rise. "Apparently from there, they have a bird's eye view of the vehicles parked in front of the cabin. They saw the Land Rover." He gave her a rueful smile. "And they guessed that it must be you."

Hope couldn't help smiling. She loved knowing that he must have told them about her, talked about her. "And?"

"And first he asked if they should come down and introduce themselves." He laughed. "Just to wind me up. And then," he met her gaze, "he told me that he's organized the guys to cover for me tomorrow, so I don't need to go to work."

She grinned. "You don't?"

He shook his head. "Nope. So, I guess at least for tomorrow, I can be on vacation with you. If you want to hang out with me, that is."

She rubbed her chin. "Umm, I suppose I could. I haven't had time to make any other plans yet." She laughed. "Of course, I want to hang out with you! That's why I came up here. I don't want to get in the way, though. If you need to work, you should. I can wait."

"No, I can take tomorrow. I want to." He smiled at her. "We can get up early, go out for a drive if you want."

"I'd love to." She loved the idea of waking up with him, more than whatever they might do with the day.

He came to her and offered her his hand, pulling her up from her seat. "If we're going to get up early, we should probably get to bed early, right?"

She laughed and slapped his gorgeous butt. "We should, definitely."

Chapter Nine

Chance opened his eyes and smiled. His arm was wrapped tightly around Hope. She was still here. It hadn't been a dream; he hadn't made it up. She was here. She'd come to Montana, come to him, and this morning here she was in his bed, sleeping on beside him. Her hair fanned out on the pillow around her. Damn. She was beautiful. She was warm and soft and ... no, he didn't need to wake her up like that. He could just lie here beside her for a while, enjoy being with her. It felt so good, and at the same time alien to him to wake up beside a woman. He and Chloe had been kids. They'd rarely gotten to spend an entire night together; he usually had to get her home before daybreak. Chance closed his eyes and sighed. He shouldn't let his mind stray back to her. It made him feel guilty like he was cheating on her.

When he opened his eyes again, Hope was looking up at him, a little crease furrowing her brow. "Are you thinking about Chloe?"

He nodded, now he felt twice as bad—like he was cheating on Hope. Damn, he was screwed up. He didn't know what to say.

Hope smiled. "I wish I could have met her."

Wow, that was the last thing he'd expected her to say. "I think you two would have gotten along." It was weird to think about the two of them coming face-too-face, but he knew they

would have liked each other. Chloe had been fun,
straightforward, full of life just like Hope was.

"Probably, we have the same taste in men."

He smiled. "I feel bad thinking about her when I'm with you,
but I feel bad being with you and not thinking about her."

"I think I can understand that, but please don't feel bad
thinking about her. I don't see her as competition for your
attention. It's like I told you before, she's a part of you. She
made you who you are, and I'm grateful to her."

Chance tightened his arm around her and drew her closer.
"Thank you."

"I'm not saying it for you. I'm saying it because it's true."

He nodded, not knowing what else to say, or even what to
think.

Hope smiled. "Are you going to make me some coffee? If
we're going to get an early start, we'd better get moving."

Just like that, she moved things forward. He might have stayed
stuck in a conversation about Chloe and how mixed up he
was, wanting to explain things to her. Hope was more
interested in getting on with this day. In living in the moment.
It wasn't that she didn't care; he knew she did, but she was
realistic. They weren't going to change anything by talking
about it—only time would make a difference. He still didn't
want to let go of Chloe's memory, but it seemed, as far as
Hope was concerned, he didn't need to. He just needed time
to get used to having room for both of them, in his mind and
in his heart. Right now, neither of them were really in his life.
He smiled and sat up. "Yes, ma'am. One pot of good, strong
coffee coming up."

She leaned over and planted a kiss on his chest. "Thank you;
I'll go take a shower."

He raised an eyebrow when she came into the kitchen wearing the same clothes she'd had on yesterday. "Do we need to take you back to get changed?"

She shrugged. "If we're heading that way, I'd like to stop in, but if we're not, I'll survive. I shouldn't smell too bad now I've had a shower."

He laughed. "You know, I would have had you down as a pampered princess, but you're not, are you?"

She laughed with him. "Nope, I've never been one of those." Her smile faded. "I think before I met you, I was guilty of getting a little too self-absorbed, but I've always had to be pretty self-reliant. I come from privilege, I won't deny that, but I've never been pampered."

"Aww." He poured her a mug of coffee and took it to her. "Here, I don't really know how pampering works, but I made you coffee."

She took it and reached up to plant a kiss on his lips. "You're the sweetest. Thank you."

Chance narrowed his eyes at her. "Sweet?"

She laughed. "Yes, sweet."

He looked over his shoulder. "Don't let anyone hear you say that, will you?"

"I think they probably already know you've got it in you, no matter how hard you try to hide it behind the badass exterior."

"So, I'm sweet, but I'm a badass?"

"I guess so. I think we're all walking contradictions when you think about it."

"I guess we are." He picked up his coffee. "I'm going to jump in the shower. I won't be long."

~ ~ ~

When he'd gone, Hope took her coffee outside onto the back porch and sat down. She loved the early morning in Montana. It was still chilly, the air was crisp, and the sky was blue. She sipped her coffee and looked out at the mountains. They were the same mountains that had provided the backdrop to her childhood. They looked a little different from down here; the ranch was much farther down the valley than the house where she'd grown up. It felt right somehow that she should be back here. Everything was the same, but she was seeing it from a slightly different perspective. She sighed and took another sip of her coffee—that was a little deep for this early in the morning.

She tensed when she heard footsteps approaching. Hopefully, they were going to the front door, and she'd be able to hide out back here unnoticed. No such luck. The sound of boots on gravel grew louder as they came around the cabin and then stopped.

That was one big, tall, handsome cowboy!

"Good morning to you, Miss Hope." He smiled. It was such a warm, open, friendly smile that she couldn't help smiling back.

She wasn't certain, but she risked a guess. "Good morning to you, Mr. Shane."

His smile widened. "How did you know I was me?"

She laughed at the way he put it. "I didn't know, but from the way Chance described you, I figured you must be you."

Shane grinned and came around to the porch steps. He held his hand out, and she stood to shake it. "Shane Remington. It's a real pleasure to meet you."

"It's a pleasure to meet you, too. Hope Davenport, though you already knew that."

"I did. I'm so happy to see you here."

"Thank you. I'm happy to be here."

The door opened behind her, and she turned to see Chance standing there, his eyes narrowed at Shane.

"Good morning!" Hope could tell by the way he grinned at Chance that there was a whole conversation going on unspoken between them.

"Morning, yourself. I see you two have met."

"We have. I was just telling Hope how happy I am that she's here."

Chance laughed and turned to Hope. "You should probably know that this guy has been my agony aunt the last couple of days."

She smiled and looked at Shane. "Thank you."

"The pleasure's all mine. I would have helped out sooner, but he didn't want to talk to anyone at all when he first came back from Oregon." He winked at her, making her chuckle. "You'll have to watch him; he can be a bit broody and silent sometimes."

"I'd noticed that. Do you have any advice on how to handle it?" She looked at Chance, glad to see that his eyes were smiling, even though he was trying to scowl at Shane.

Shane shrugged. "I haven't figured it out myself yet. It usually just takes time."

"I'm not so bad." Chance smiled at her.

She went to stand beside him, and he wrapped his arm around her shoulders. "No, you're not bad at all, except when you're leaving notes and sneaking out in the middle of the night."

Shane laughed out loud. "I don't think you need any advice from me, Hope. You just call him on his crap, and you should be able to keep him in line, no problem."

Chance hugged her closer to him and smiled through pursed lips. "Are you two going to gang up on me, just when I'm trying to open up and trust you?"

Hope slapped his arm. "Don't you go twisting it all around and making yourself the victim," she said with a laugh.

She was surprised by the serious look he gave Shane. "I'll try not to. Apparently, it's a bad habit of mine."

Shane shook his head. "It's not a habit, just something you need to watch out for."

Hope liked but didn't understand the look they exchanged. They were obviously touching on a subject that had come up between them before. Chance seemed grateful to Shane, and Shane seemed to be encouraging him. She already knew she loved the relationship they had.

"And what are you doing here, anyway?" asked Chance.

Shane grinned again. "I was going to make up some bull-crap story about needing to talk to you or needing to borrow a cup of sugar or something." He winked at Hope again. "But we all know I just had to come over here to meet the lovely Hope and to tell you both how happy I am that you're here."

Hope smiled, loving his honesty.

Chance smiled too and grasped his shoulder. "Thanks, though it's a good thing Hope isn't the kind to get embarrassed by you doing that."

Shane grinned at her. "I doubt she'd be hanging out with you if she were the type to get embarrassed by much of anything."

She laughed, and Chance looked at her. "Sorry, but he has kind of got a point."

"I suppose." He turned back to Shane. "Do I need to get you coffee so we can all sit and visit?"

"No! I'm not going to hold you up, I'm sure the two of you have better things to do with your day, and besides, I need to get to work. I just couldn't resist coming over to say hi." He tipped his hat at Hope. "It's a real pleasure. I'll look forward to seeing you again soon."

"You too."

He grinned at Chance before making his way back down the steps. "Have a great day, Chancey."

Hope laughed at the look on Chance's face as Shane disappeared around the side of the cabin. "Chancey?"

He scowled at her. "It's what little Ruby calls me."

"I like it, but I'll bet she's the only one who can get away with it?"

Chance pursed his lips. "Her and my sister, Missy."

Hope couldn't help but laugh at the look on his face. "I take it you won't be too happy if I start calling you my sweet Chancey, then?"

His eyes narrowed, and his arm snaked around her waist pulling her to him. "You wouldn't dare."

She smiled up at him. "Oh, wouldn't I?"

He shook his head grimly and lowered his head to gently bite her bottom lip. "You'd better not."

"Ooh, that sounds like a threat to me. What are you going to do to stop me?"

He raised an eyebrow and held her closer, so close she could feel his heart beating in his muscular chest. "Do you really want to find out?"

She could feel how hard he was as he crushed her against him. She nodded. "I think I do."

He shook his head and let her go. "Maybe we should just consider this a warning."

She laughed. "We could, or you could go through with it, show me what you want to do about it." For a moment there, she'd been sure he was going to take her back inside and make love to her.

"Do you really want to spend the day in bed? It's a coin toss for me, at this point. I'm trying to be a gentleman, and take you out for the day instead, but if you keep pushing, my resolve's not going to last much longer."

Hope thought about it. She'd love to spend the day in bed with him, but she'd rather spend the time getting to know each other better—as people, not just getting to know each other's bodies better. She sighed. "Okay, let's get out of here before my resolve is gone, too."

Before they got into Chance's truck, he shot a look over at the Land Rover. "Do you want to take that back? I can follow you up there if you do."

"No." Hope wanted to head down to the park from here. She didn't want to waste time going back to up to Oscar's place or running into Uncle Johnny and Aunt Jean. She wasn't worried about them seeing her with Chance; quite the opposite, in fact. She was more worried that if they ran into them, they'd have to spend at least some time with them, and she wanted Chance all to herself. She smiled at him. "I'd rather leave it here. That way I can decide for myself when I'm ready to leave. Unless you don't want it on show here?"

He smirked. "It's a bit late for that. I told you last night; they'd all know you were here within five minutes of your arrival. It can stay here forever as far as I'm concerned."

Hope sucked in a deep breath. Did he mean that the way it sounded? She looked up to meet his gaze, but he'd left her side and was on his way around to the driver's door. He climbed in and waited for her to join him.

She gave him a puzzled look as she fastened her seat belt, but he didn't meet her gaze. He couldn't have meant it that way. She was just reading too much into his words. Hell, last night she'd even imagined that he'd said he loved her! She needed to get a grip. Wherever things were going between them, they weren't going that fast. For both their sakes, they needed to go slowly and tread carefully.

He gave her a bright smile as he pulled away. "Have you ever had breakfast at Mammoth Hot Springs?"

"Not for years and years. We used to go down there sometimes when I was little."

"Want to go back?"

"I'd love to."

He smiled at her as he pulled out of the driveway. "This is going to be fun."

"It is. You surprise me that you'd go down to the park as a tourist."

He shrugged. "I love it. Not the touristy parts. I rarely get down there in the summer months, it's too busy for my taste, but sometimes, I'll go. Mason, Shane, and I have been known to go camping in the backcountry."

"That much I can see, but I don't picture you stopping in at Mammoth on the way."

He turned and narrowed his eyes at her, smiling even though he was trying to look tough. "Okay, spoil it then, why don't you? I'm trying to impress you here. I asked if you wanted to go to the hotel. I never have. I know the girls like it. They go down there sometimes, just for a fun, fancy breakfast. I was trying to impress you, but it looks like I've blown it."

She leaned over and kissed his cheek. "No, you haven't. That's so sweet of you." He made a face that had her laughing again. "I'm sorry, but it is!"

He shrugged and fixed his eyes on the road ahead.

She prodded his arm. "Are you mad at me?"

He shook his head. "Nope, I'm just trying to do the badass stare and remind you I'm not a wuss."

She laughed. "No one could ever accuse you of that. You should take me calling you sweet as a compliment. I'm not saying you're a pussy; I'm saying you're kind-hearted and thoughtful."

He turned to look at her. "Yeah?"

She laughed. "Yes! Sweet doesn't mean weak in any way. In fact, for a guy, I'd say you have to have a certain kind of strength before you can be sweet."

"In that case, I'll take it." He smirked to himself as he drove on.

"You'll take it, but what?" she asked with a laugh. "I can tell there's a but."

"But I still don't want you to let anyone else hear you say it."

She laughed. "I wouldn't worry if I were you. Like I told you, I think they already know."

Chapter Ten

Chance was happy to let Hope go ahead of him as they entered the dining room at the hotel. Not only was he pleased to be there with her, as her man, but doing the gentlemanly thing of letting her enter ahead of him gave him a minute to lurk behind her and figure out the lay of the land. She'd been right. This wasn't his usual scene at all. He didn't know why people liked to get all dressed up and go out and eat in a place where seeing and being seen was as much a part of the meal as the food. He'd rather stay home and grill out on the back porch, even fry up some bacon and eggs and take them outside to eat in the fresh air with a view of the mountains. He'd rather watch herds of cattle while he ate than herds of humans jostling over a breakfast buffet.

Hope turned to smile at him when they reached the hostess station.

"Two of you?" the girl asked.

Chance stepped forward and took his hat off as he nodded. "Yeah …"

"Actually, I think we need to hang back," said Hope with a smile. The girl gave her an enquiring look, as Hope gestured to the couple behind them in line to go by. She smiled. "We're waiting for people."

The girl nodded and smiled to greet her next guests. Chance frowned at Hope, wondering what her problem might be and hoping that she hadn't spotted someone with a camera pointed in her direction again. He stepped closer, feeling as though he needed to protect her from some unknown threat.

She slipped her hand into his and tugged him back outside. Chance raised an eyebrow when she finally reached the end of the long line they'd just waited in. "What's the problem?"

She smiled. "None, now."

"What was it, though? Why did you say we're waiting for people?"

She laughed. "Because we don't need to be in there. It was sweet of you to think of it, and I can see why the girls would enjoy it, but it's not your kind of place, is it?"

He shook his head, feeling bad that he must have made it so obvious. "No, but I could've ... I would've."

"Aww." She stood on tiptoe and planted a kiss on his lips. "I know, and I love you for it."

Chance's heart stopped beating for a moment. Did she realize what she'd just said? Apparently, not.

"But we don't need to spend our time in there on a beautiful day like this, not when only one of us would enjoy it."

"I'd enjoy seeing you enjoy it."

"I know, but if we stop in the souvenir shop and pick up a sandwich, we can find a nice quiet spot out in the fresh air somewhere and both enjoy it."

He pursed his lips.

"Am I right, or am I right?"

He smiled grudgingly. "You're right, just like always."

She laughed and slipped her arm through his, leading him away from the restaurant and toward the souvenir shop. "I'm glad you're a fast learner. The sooner you understand that about me, the better we'll do!"

He had to laugh at her audacity. "You reckon that's how this is going to work, do you?"

She nodded, trying not to laugh. "Of course. Do you have a problem with that?"

He shook his head. "Nope, no problem. You can think you're right all of the time, and I'll just work around it."

"And how do you think you're going to do that?"

He grinned and bent down, wrapping his arms around her thighs, and throwing her over his shoulder before she even knew what he was doing. He set off toward the souvenir shop, laughing as she paddled his ass shouting, "Put me down!"

"Nope."

He could feel her laughing as he went. People turned to look at them, but he didn't care. They were having fun. It surprised him that most of the people who looked their way smiled. One guy met his eye and winked. An older lady with a backpack and hiking boots stopped and grinned at him; then she bent down to address Hope. "Don't spank him too hard, dear. He might return the favor later." Chance couldn't help but laugh as she straightened up and spoke to him. "Or is that the plan?" she asked with a gleam in her eye.

When he reached the souvenir store, he let Hope slide gently down to her feet.

Her cheeks were pink as she looked up at him. She was still laughing. "I should be mad at you for that."

"Yeah, but you're not, are you?"

She shook her head, and he leaned down to land a gentle kiss on her plump pink lips. "Good."

Inside the store, they picked up sandwiches and chips. Chance smiled to himself as Hope eyed the trinkets on the counter while they waited in line at the cash register.

"What?" she asked when she caught him watching her.

"All those knick-knacks; I can never believe that people really buy them. I mean, what's the point?"

She shook her head sadly and heaved out an exaggerated sigh.

"Oh, my poor, sweet Chancey."

He scowled at her, and she laughed.

"You really don't get it?"

He shook his head.

"Well, that's just sad."

"Why? I think it's sad that people pay way too much for things they don't even need, just because they're here."

"They don't pay too much; they're not paying for keyrings and fridge magnets and all these other things that you see."

"So, what are they paying for? All I see is people being charged ten bucks for little hunks of plastic and metal, just because they've got the word Yellowstone on them."

She sighed again. "Have you ever been on vacation?"

"What do you mean?"

"I mean, have you ever gone to visit a place, just because you wanted to see it, to enjoy being there?"

"No, I don't suppose I have."

"I didn't think so. Which is why you don't see the value in these little souvenirs." She picked up a key ring and dangled the plastic bear in front of him. "See this? This isn't a bear or a key ring. This is a memory, or at least a token, a memento. When these people go back home, wherever home may be, they go back to their lives and their jobs. On a cold dark rainy morning next January, someone who bought one of these key rings will see it when they lock up their house on their way out to work. They'll see this little bear, and they'll smile, remembering what a good time they had here. This little hunk of plastic and metal will bring a smile to their face as they remember what a great time they had today. It will be a bright spot in a dark day, in the middle of winter. It'll remind them of happy times, and give them hope of more happy times ahead, next time they get to go on vacation."

Chance stared at her. It made sense. He understood what she was saying, understood the sentiment, though he'd never have thought of it that way. He nodded slowly and smiled. "I stand corrected. Thank you."

She smiled back. "You're most welcome."

They reached the head of the line and Chance took her sandwich from her and put everything together on the counter.

"Is that everything?" asked the girl as she rang them up on the cash register.

Chance smiled and turned back to the carousel displaying the keyrings. He selected two grizzly bears and handed them over. "I'll take these, as well."

Hope gave him a puzzled look, but he just shrugged and paid the girl.

When they got back outside, he opened up the plastic bag and took out the bears. He examined them closely, then handed one to Hope.

"Thank you." She was still looking puzzled, waiting for him to explain.

"That one's the prettier of the two," he said with a smile. "Look, it's got longer eyelashes, it's the girl."

She laughed and gave it back to him. "In that case, I want the boy. The gruff and grumpy one, to remind me of you."

Chance handed it over. "Okay."

They started walking back to the truck. "Why did you buy them, when you think it's such a silly idea?" asked Hope. She was stroking the little bear and smiling.

"I don't think it's silly now. Not now you've explained it to me. I like the idea. And ..." Oh, what the hell, he may as well say it. "I like the idea of having a little memento of you, something that will make me smile and remember this day, whenever I see it."

She nodded, looking thoughtful. "I like that idea, too."

They reached the truck, and he opened the passenger door for her.

"What's the matter?" he asked when he got into the driver's seat. "I thought it was a nice idea. Sweet, even," he added, in an attempt to make her smile again.

It worked, but it was a weak smile. "It is, it's a lovely idea. It's just that, come January, I don't want to be left with a little bear who reminds me of you. I'd rather still have you."

He met her gaze and nodded. "I would, too."

She leaned toward him, and he slid his fingers into her hair, pulling her closer for a kiss that he never wanted to end. When it finally did, there were tears glistening in her eyes.

"I'm sorry."

Chance caught his breath. "What for?"

"For being greedy, for asking too much, for not keeping it light and casual, for talking about the future, when all that's on offer is the next two weeks."

He drew her closer so he could wrap his arm around her shoulders. "That's not all that's on offer. I want more, too, honey. I want it all, but I don't know if I'm cut out for it. I'm trying to keep it light, trying not to pile on the pressure—on you or me—because I don't want to let you down. I don't want to say I will, only to find out I can't."

She nodded into his chest. "You don't make promises, right?"

"I haven't. Not for eighteen years. Promises can do a lot of damage when they're broken, and even more damage if they're kept."

She sat up and smiled. "I know. I'm sorry. We're supposed to be no promises and no regrets. Right now, you're probably regretting getting me my little bear." She held it up and dangled it in front of his face. "But I love him; he's so sweet." Chance rolled his eyes, and she laughed. "He is. I may just have to call him my Chancey bear."

He narrowed his eyes at her.

"But right now, I think we should get out of here. I bet you know some place we can go to sit and eat our sandwiches in peace and just take in how beautiful this place is."

Chance started up the engine. There was so much more he wanted to say, so much more he wanted to offer her, to share with her, but not until he knew he could. Until he was sure he was capable of giving her what she wanted, he'd probably do better to keep his mouth shut. He smiled, deciding it best to follow her lead and lighten the mood and move on. "I know the perfect spot; I think you'll love it."

~ ~ ~

It was late by the time they drove out of the north gate of the park. Chance had been true to his word and taken her to a beautiful spot to eat their breakfast. She'd felt like they were dining on top of the world and was glad that she'd decided to leave the restaurant before they were seated.

They'd driven on down through the park. He'd asked if she wanted to stop to see Old Faithful, but she'd seen it hundreds of times. She was still fascinated by the work of nature, but she was less enthralled at the prospect of sitting around with hundreds of other people waiting for the geyser to blow. She made him promise that he'd bring her back early one morning so they could visit as close to daybreak as they could. She'd done that with her mom once, and it was a memory she treasured.

Chance looked over at her. "Do you want to stop for a burger before we head back?"

"Sure." They hadn't eaten since their sandwich at breakfast. "Can we stop into the grocery store, too? I should pick up a toothbrush and some toiletries."

Chance grinned. "You bet. Had we better get you a souvenir T-shirt and sweatpants, too? I know you're not a pampered princess, but three days in the same clothes might be a bit much."

"Yeah, we should. Although I'm going to have to go back up to Oscar's tomorrow." She couldn't help it; she was pleased to see his grin fade. "You can come, if you like?"

"I'm going to have to get back to work tomorrow. I could come up and see you when I get done? You can visit with your aunt and uncle during the day, and then I won't feel so bad hogging your time in the evening."

"That works. Everybody wins."

It felt strange wandering up and down the aisles of the grocery store with him. She wasn't much into domesticity, let alone shared domesticity, but this was good. She didn't miss the way women eyed him as he went by. He was one good-looking cowboy, no doubt about it. She took hold of his hand, and he smiled down at her. He was her cowboy. At least he was for now. How realistic was it to think he could be hers forever? That she wouldn't be left with just memories and a little bear? She had to get a grip. She didn't want to waste the moment she was in by wondering about moments that might or might not come. Who knew what was realistic between her and Chance? Only time would tell.

When their basket was full of toiletries and some cookies and other goodies she'd thrown in, they paid and made their way back to the truck.

Chance turned to her after he'd put the bags on the backseat. He looked so serious, she was worried. "What is it?"

He smiled. "I think I get it, about the key rings and the memories. Do you remember the first time we were in a grocery store together?"

She frowned, thinking that this was the first time.

"In Oregon. That first day we met." He smirked. "After you tried to ram me in the parking lot, we both went to the same grocery store. You were behind me when I was checking out."

"Of course! And the girl on the cash register was so busy mooning over you; I thought I'd never get out of there."

He narrowed his eyes at her. "And when you did get out of there, you ignored me. I'd decided I was going to smile at you, maybe even wave. You were going to be my first attempt at being friendly to a stranger, but you just stuck your nose in the air and walked on by. You got in your car and drove away without even looking in my direction."

She had to laugh. "You need to observe a little more closely. I watched you sitting in your car; I was eyeing you up the whole way. That's one thing about those big glasses. I can look, but as long as I don't look like I'm looking, no one ever knows."

"So, you did notice me?"

She nodded. "Oh boy, did I!"

He laughed. "So, we can count that as our official first meeting?"

"We can. Especially if it means we don't have to talk about me not paying attention when I was
backing out of my space at the clinic."

"Yeah, we probably shouldn't talk about that. I didn't think much of that near miss."

She nodded. She didn't always pay enough attention when she was driving. "Sorry."

"I thought we weren't going to talk about it?"

She laughed. "About what? Now, are we going to get a burger? I seem to remember there's a place here in Gardiner that does an elk burger."

"There is, that's the place I was going to suggest."

Chapter Eleven

Chance urged Rio on. They were driving the herd to the higher pasture now that it was turning green everywhere. In a few weeks, it'd be time to move the cattle up to the summertime pasture. He watched Brad rein his horse around and bring in a couple of strays who broke away. Chance should have gotten to them first, but he wasn't focusing as he should be today.

"Thanks, Brad," he called.

Brad turned and nodded. He had the same glint in his eye all the guys had had all morning. Chance knew they were dying to ask about Hope. More likely they wanted to tease him, but none of them would dare do that. He wasn't well known for his sense of humor when it came to anything personal. What the hell, though. If he was making efforts to be friendlier to strangers, shouldn't he be doing the same with the guys he worked with? He smiled. "Go on, say it, my head is obviously elsewhere."

Brad smirked. "I'd love to say it, but I don't want my head bitten off."

Rick rode around to join them. "I'm used to getting mine bitten off." He grinned at Chance. "So, I'll say it. You'd be better off leaving us to take care of the herd today. You should get back to taking care of your fancy lady."

Chance narrowed his eyes at him. He did tend to give Rick a
hard time, but he shouldn't do it now. The guy was only
picking up on an opening Chance had given them. He smiled.
"I'd love to, but I figured I couldn't leave you alone for two
days in a row."

Rick laughed. "If a girl like that was here to see me, I'd leave
you all alone for two months in a row!"

Brad nodded. "You should make the most of the time you've
got. How long is she going to be here? I can keep ole Ricky in
line."

"She's going back in a couple of weeks."

Brad met his eye, seeming to understand.

Rick's eyes widened. "So, why the hell are you out here with
us? You should get back to her, get her back in the sack while
you still can."

Chance pressed his lips together, glad they were on horseback
right now. If he could've reached Rick, he would have
punched him.

Brad solved the situation neatly by slapping Rick's horse on
the rear, making the mare lunge forward. "Zip it, Rick. You're
talking about a lady, so watch your mouth. She's not like the
girls you coax into your truck and out of their panties after the
dive bar in town."

Rick gave Chance a rueful grin over his shoulder as he rode
away. "Sorry, boss. I didn't think. I didn't realize this was the
real deal. I'd better start talking a bit nicer to you if you're
going to be marrying into the zillionaire Davenport family,
huh?"

Chance shook his head as he watched Rick ride to the back of
the herd to round up the stragglers.

"Is it serious, serious?" asked Brad as they rode side by side
through the gate.

Chance shrugged. "I don't do serious." What else could he say?

"But if you did, would this be serious?"

Chance nodded. "It would."

Brad grinned. "I'll keep 'em crossed for you then."

"Look who's coming," called Rick.

Chance looked to where he was pointing. A big gray gelding was cantering across the top pasture, coming down to meet them. Both the horse and his rider were immediately recognizable. Chance smiled and watched Carter come closer. He grinned when he reached them. "Hey."

"Hey. What are you doing out here?"

"Getting some fresh air, and some exercise with my old buddy here."

"Good for you."

Carter smiled sheepishly. "And, of course, hoping I might run into you. Check how you're doing."

Carter liked to take care of everyone. He was the one who hung the family together. He liked to know everyone was happy, and when they weren't, he wanted to do anything he could to fix things. Chance smiled. "Thanks. I'm doing great. Hope's here."

Carter laughed. "I know that much. I want to make sure that you're happy about it. That everything's okay between the two of you. I was worried sick when I heard that there were news stories about her and Matt. I didn't know what to do. For a minute, it looked like my wife's sister and my brother were both going to get their hearts broken."

"Is Autumn seeing Matt?"

Carter shrugged. "I don't think so, not officially, I don't really know what their deal is. It's obvious they're nuts about each other, but they're too busy arguing most of the time to do anything about it."

"I hope they figure it out, but at least she has no worries about Matt when it comes to Hope."

Carter smiled. "I'm glad the two of you got past that. I know how it feels to have your private life in the papers."

Chance nodded, remembering how a story in the local press had almost ruined things for Carter and his wife Summer before they got together. "I wasn't too worried."

Carter laughed. "Yeah, it's easy to say that now, right?"

"It is." Chance didn't want to admit just how worried he'd been that Hope might have forgotten all about him and moved on—whether it was with Matt or someone else. "But it's all behind us now. She's going to be staying here for the next couple of weeks, and we plan to make the most of it."

Carter looked concerned. "You're not getting into the same kind of situation I did, are you?"

"What do you mean?"

"Summer was only supposed to be staying here for three months. After that, she was supposed to go home to Nashville and to her career. She ended up staying because she couldn't sing anymore, but for a while there, it looked like a shared future was going to be impossible for us."

Chance nodded. He hadn't really given much thought to a shared future as Carter put it. He'd thought about the logistics of Hope and him being able to see each other. With her life in LA and his here on the ranch, it'd be difficult, but not impossible. He looked Carter in the eye as he thought it over. What if they did want to share a life? What would that look like? He couldn't give up his life here and the ranch. But how could she give up her life and her business? He pressed his lips together.

Carter looked concerned. "Okay, now you know why I'm really out here. I've been where you are. It might look impossible right now, but if you both want it, you'll find a way."

Chance nodded. He didn't see that there was a way to be found, but he shrugged. "Maybe, but we're not to that point yet. We're just seeing each other, getting to know each other. There's no need to rush into the big stuff. It's fine." He gave Carter what he hoped was a reassuring smile. Judging by the concern on his face, Carter wasn't fooled.

"Whatever you say. Just remember I'm always around if you want me."

"Thanks."

"Do you want to bring her for dinner on Thursday? It's our turn to host everyone. I didn't know if you'd want to bring her, or if you'd want to skip it."

Chance sucked in a deep breath. He didn't know what he wanted to do. Part of him liked the idea of introducing Hope to the brothers and their wives—of her getting to know them, and them her. Part of him liked the idea of going to one of the family dinners with his girl by his side. But then again, another part of him thought it was a really bad idea. It would be giving himself a glimpse of what life could be like if she stayed—and knowing that she couldn't stay. He met Carter's eye. "Can I let you know?"

"Of course. That's why I wanted to ask you now. Give you time to think about it before you have to decide."

"Thanks, bud." The others might tease Carter for being so thoughtful, but he was a big guy with a big heart, and it was usually helpful; the guys just didn't like to admit that.

"You should take some time off while she's here. The guys can handle it, can't they? Is she at the cabin?"

"No, she was supposed to be staying at her cousin's house, up by Dr. Johnny's. She's gone back up there today."

"Which cousin?

"Oscar. The one who has a house up there."

Carter smiled. "They all have houses up there. Have you met them?"

"No. She hasn't talked about them much. Just said that she grew up with them. She said she'd been here for Oscar's party a couple of years ago, but it sounds like she doesn't see much of them."

"I don't know what you'll make of Oscar when you meet him. He was okay back then, a bit of a big head, but he was a lot of fun. I haven't seen him in years, but whenever he's in the news, he seems to be some kind of playboy." He smiled. "Not your kind of guy, at least not on the surface."

Chance shrugged. "I probably won't even meet him. From what Hope said he doesn't come up here much." And Chance couldn't allow himself to consider the possibility of running into Oscar anywhere else. He couldn't think about getting to know her family—why would he?

Carter smiled. "I never thought I'd meet Matt McAllen or the one and only Clay McAdam either. You just don't know what turns your life might take when you meet the right woman."

Rick shouted and waved his arm, signaling that he needed help keeping the herd together. Chance tipped his hat at Carter, glad for the excuse to end the conversation. "I'd better go help. I'll let you know about Thursday."

"Okay."

He started to ride away, then turned back. "And, Carter."

"Yeah?"

"Thanks."

~ ~ ~

Aunt Jean set a glass of lemonade down in front of Hope with a smile. "I hope you're going to tell me all about this handsome cowboy of yours. Your uncle thinks he's wonderful." Her smile faded. "But I gather your father doesn't."

Hope nodded and stared out of the window for a moment. She loved this house. She loved all the memories it held and the feeling of warmth and happiness that her aunt and uncle just seemed to generate around them. "You know what he's like," she said sadly.

Aunt Jean sat down opposite her at the table. "I do. I didn't mean to bring that up. Let's focus on the good, and worry about the obstacles later, why don't we? I've seen Chance around; he comes up to help with the cattle sometimes." She waggled her eyebrows. "He's rather yummy."

Hope had to laugh. "He's very yummy; there's no denying that."

"And from what your uncle tells me, he's a wonderful human being, too. He's decent, honest, hard-working, he has high standards. He sounds like a wonderful package."

"He is, he may be the most decent human being I've ever known."

"But he comes from the wrong side of the tracks? Is that the only problem?"

Hope shook her head sadly. "No, if that were all, then I think Dad would get over it quite quickly. There's a lot more to it than that."

"Do you want to tell me about it, or would you rather I keep my nose out and turn the conversation back to mundane tittle-tattle?"

Hope smiled. "You're no good at tittle-tattle, you don't care enough about who's who."

Aunt Jean laughed. "Or who's *doing* who. That's all the gossip ever seems to be about. I do care when it comes to you. I want to like this Chance. I'd like to meet him, though I'm certainly not going to put you under any pressure on that. But what I care most about is that you should be happy. Is he someone who can make you happy? And even if he is, are you going to be able to be happy if your father doesn't approve?"

Hope shrugged. "I don't know is the answer to all of those questions. Being with him makes me happy. He's wonderful, Aunt Jean. But it's not as simple as that. He's a great guy, but he has a sad past, and he's not entirely over it."

Aunt Jean raised an eyebrow and waited.

"His childhood sweetheart died when they were eighteen. Just when they were supposed to start their life together, her life ended, and he's never got over it. He still loves her. He never stopped wanting the life they were going to have together."

"Until now? Until he met you?"

"It seems I'm the first person he's met who's made him even consider being with someone new. But he's still struggling. Being with me makes him feel disloyal to her."

"And how does that make you feel?"

"It doesn't hurt me. I'm not jealous of her or anything. He seems to think that I will be, but I'm not. He thinks he needs to leave her behind before he could move forward with me, but I disagree. I don't think he can ever leave her behind, nor should he. She's a part of him; she helped make him who he is." She shrugged. "I don't understand what it's like to lose your partner, the person that you love that way. But I think I do understand a little bit. I couldn't ever give up my mom."

Aunt Jean nodded and patted her hand. "I know; you shouldn't have to, and Chance shouldn't have to give up the girl that he lost, but I think many women would feel threatened by her memory. No one wants to feel like a second choice. Is that your father's problem with it all?"

Hope shook her head vigorously. "No. I don't think he's even considered the feelings involved. Dad has a problem that Chance isn't from money, or even famous. It pisses me off that he didn't mind Drew, but that's beside the point. Dad's problem is that he found out what Chance did after Chloe died." She met her aunt's gaze, wondering what she might think, but the kindness she saw in her eyes gave her the answer—Aunt Jean would understand. "You see, Chloe drowned. She went out on the lake at night with another guy after she and Chance had a fight. The next morning, the guy brought the boat back in, but Chloe was gone. Chance never believed it was an accident. When he saw the guy again months later, he beat him up—very badly. He was sent to prison, and from what he told me, he just made it worse for himself while he was in there. He didn't care about anything anymore and did more bad things, fighting and such that got his sentence extended."

"He told you all of this himself?"

Hope nodded. "He did. He knows he did wrong, but …."

"But what?"

"But if he were put in the same situation, he'd do the same thing again. He has strong protective instincts—maybe a little too strong. If someone threatens or hurts someone he cares about, he can't let it go."

"That's what he's told you, or what you've found?"

Hope shrugged. "A little of both, I guess."

"Have you ever felt afraid?"

"Oh, my goodness, no. Not for myself, at least, but he went after the man who took the photos of us in Oregon, and yeah, I was a little scared of what he was going to do to him."

Aunt Jean looked thoughtful.

"What do you think?"

"I think you've got a tough road ahead of you, dear."

Hope chuckled. "Tell me something I don't know. But that's if there even is a road ahead for us. All we've committed to is spending time together for the next few weeks, while I'm here."

"That's all anyone can ever really commit to, no matter what we think or what we say. We never know what's around the next corner."

"I know, all we can do is make the most of today. I've tried to live by that since Mom died. Chance has made me want to think about tomorrow, though." She met her aunt's gaze. "He's the first person who's made me want to think about the rest of my life."

Aunt Jean reached across and patted her hand. "I thought as much. I know I said I don't want to push you, but I'd like to meet him."

"I'd like that, too."

"And how long do you think you'll stay?"

"I've said a couple of weeks. That's what I told Toby. They don't really need me in the office or anything."

"And what will you and Chance do when you go back to LA?" Hope shrugged. "I have no idea. His whole life is here. He doesn't get a lot of time off, but he's said he would come visit me. I can take as much time as I like, but it doesn't seem right to just come up here and hang around, you know?"

"Could you move here?"

The question surprised her. "Honestly? I could. It's not like I couldn't pop back to LA whenever I'm needed, but what would I do?"

"That's what you need to think about, isn't it? It's all very well hoping for a future with him, but what kind of future might be possible? I know you don't want to get carried away this early in your friendship with him, but I think you need to decide quite soon whether there's a future worth getting carried away about."

Hope nodded. It was true. She couldn't go letting her imagination run wild about what might happen between her and Chance without giving some real thought to what a shared future might look like.

They both looked up at the sound of the front door opening. Uncle Johnny came into the den where they were sitting. "Oh, dear. What are the glum faces about?"

Hope smiled. "Nothing, just pondering life, the universe, and everything."

Uncle Johnny chuckled. "And let me guess, everything includes a certain cowboy in a black hat?"

"Yeah, you know me too well."

He came and patted her shoulder. "I do. I know that you'll work it out and I hope you know that you'll have our support."

She smiled up at him. "Thanks. That's one thing I've always known, and I love you both for it." She got to her feet. "I'm going to go back down to Oscar's and let you get on with your evening."

Uncle Johnny smiled. "Have a good evening yourself. Is he coming here or are you going back down there?"

"He's coming up here this evening."

"Ooh, don't be too surprised if you see me out for a walk later, then," said Aunt Jean with a smile.

Hope laughed. "I won't."

Chapter Twelve

Chance smiled to himself as he turned into the driveway at Dr. Johnny's place. He'd been here often enough in the past, but that was always to help with the cattle. This was different. Tonight, he was here to see Hope, and he couldn't wait. He slowed the truck as he approached the big house. Dr. Johnny and his wife were sitting out on the porch. He put his window down and brought the truck to a stop. As much as he couldn't wait to get to Hope, he felt he needed to say hi to them. He also wanted to get a feel for their reaction to him. Johnny had been brusque with him on the phone last time they'd talked. He didn't know Mrs. Davenport, other than to wave to. He hoped she didn't disapprove of Hope seeing a ranch hand. There was only one way to find out.

"Evening," he called.

"Hey, Chance." Johnny grinned at him. "She's down at Oscar's place. You know which one it is, don't you?"

"I do, thanks." He smiled at Mrs. Davenport. "Nice to see you, ma'am."

He was relieved when she smiled back and gave him a little wave. "Not as nice as it is to see you. Go on, she's waiting for you, and if you linger around here, I'll only invite you both up for a drink so I can get to know you."

Chance smiled. "I'll go bring her up if you'd like?"

Mrs. Davenport shook her head with a laugh. "That's very sweet of you, but I don't think Hope would be too pleased with me. Perhaps another time? You two enjoy your evening."

"I'd get out of here while you can, if I were you." said Johnny with a grin.

Chance tipped his hat to them and carried on down the lane. He'd wanted to see how they reacted to him. He couldn't have hoped for better than that.

Hope was standing on the front steps waiting for him when he pulled up. Oscar's place was pretty grand, especially considering he only used it a couple of weeks a year. Hope looked perfectly at home standing there in front of the huge oak door.

She came down the steps to greet him when he got out of the truck. "Hey. Did you have a nice day at the office, dear?"

He laughed. "It was an okay day. The cows and the horses mostly behaved themselves; the hands were a bit rowdy, but nothing I couldn't handle. The roughest part of the day was that it took so long."

She smiled. "Mine dragged. I missed you."

He wrapped his arm around her shoulders and drew her to him. "I missed you, too, honey."

She looked up to meet his gaze. For a moment her eyes were full of questions, then they were gone. She nodded as if to dismiss them. "Well, you're here now, and that's all that really matters. Come on in. I hope you're hungry; I made us a big salad and a lasagna."

He raised his eyebrows. "You cook?"

She laughed. "Yes, I cook. I enjoy it. I couldn't cook in Oregon, because of my ankle. I couldn't stand around the kitchen on it for too long." She took his hand and led him inside. "I hope you'll like it. I almost called to ask if you even eat lasagna, but …" she turned to look up at him, "I didn't want to be that chick who bugs you at work, calling all the time to ask about nothing."

Chance laughed. "You can call me any time you want to. I'd love it. I thought about calling you a bunch of times today, but I didn't have anything to say. I just wanted to hear your voice."

The way she smiled told him how much that pleased her. "You don't need to have anything to say. I just want to hear your voice, too."

They stood there staring into each other's eyes for a long moment. Chance's heart clenched in his chest. She was so beautiful, and she already meant so much to him. He'd never have believed that he was the kind of guy who'd want to call a girl, just to hear her, or stand around like this looking deep into her eyes.

She gave a brief nod. "Sorry, I'm going all sappy on you here. Come on into the kitchen, and I'll fix you a drink while I dish up dinner."

Chance gave himself a shake when she turned away to open the fridge. If she was going all sappy, he seemed to have it even worse.

They sat on the deck behind the house to eat. This had to be the most beautiful view of the valley he'd seen—and he considered every inch of this valley to be beautiful. "This is quite a place Oscar's got here."

Hope nodded. "He has good taste, expensive taste, in everything. From houses to cars to women. Oscar has to have the best and he doesn't mind paying for it."

Chance picked up the bottle of wine, happy to see that it was the same Cab Franc he'd bought for her in Oregon. He filled her glass and waited for her to start eating before he picked up his own fork. "And does he work? Does he earn all this money he spends, or is it family money?"

Hope laughed. "God, no! Oscar is a serial entrepreneur. He's built and sold at least half a dozen companies that I can think of. He's some kind of genius. He's like the bright kid at school who's so clever he gets all the work done too fast and then has so much time and creativity left over that he goes and gets himself into mischief."

Chance nodded.

"Didn't you say your brother-in-law built up and sold a tech company in Silicon Valley?"

Chance smiled at the thought of Dan. "Yeah. He's a genius, no doubt about it. It doesn't sound like he's anything like your Oscar, though. Dan's quiet, unassuming. He's a computer nerd, through and through."

"Really? From what you've told me about your sister, I wouldn't have expected her to be with a guy like that."

Chance chuckled. "Neither would I. They couldn't be more different if they tried, but they're perfect for each other. They're each what the other needs. And Dan's been the best thing that could ever have happened to my nephew Scot."

"You really love the kids in your life, don't you?"

"What do you mean?"

"It's obvious, whenever you mention Scot or little Ruby, your face kind of lights up and you look softer."

He shrugged. "I guess I do love them. They're both awesome kids."

"Have you ever thought about having kids of your own?"

Chance nearly choked on his salad and put his fork down.

Hope laughed. "Sorry, I didn't mean anything by it, I just wondered, while we were on the subject."

Chance shook his head. "Until I met you I haven't even thought about being with a woman, let alone being a dad."

"I should have known that. Sorry, but for what it's worth, I think you'd be an amazing father."

Chance nodded. He didn't know what to say. Kids of his own weren't something he'd considered a possibility.

"Okay. Let's change the subject, shall we? I seem to be good at opening my mouth just to put my foot in it."

He chuckled. "Not so fast. Have you ever thought about having kids?"

Her eyes widened in surprise at the question, but she didn't answer immediately.

Chance waited. It was important to him now to know what she thought.

Eventually, she sighed. "I try not to think about it. When I was younger, kids weren't a priority. I had my career, I didn't have a man in my life, and I felt like I had all the time in the world. These last few years, though ..." she shrugged. "I'm not getting any younger, am I? I guess I've started to feel like my time has passed—and that makes me feel like I've missed out on something that would have been very important to me." She shrugged again.

"Too old? At thirty-three? I'm thirty-six."

"Yeah, but it's different for guys, isn't it?"

"I suppose so, but not much. If we had a kid this year, I'd be fifty-five before they were eighteen, and you'd be ..." The way she was looking at him made him stop. He realized that he was talking about them having a child together.

"Hypothetically speaking, of course."

He nodded. "Of course." He took a big gulp of his wine. What the hell was he thinking? He was relieved when his phone started to ring in his pocket. He wasn't going to answer it, but at least it provided a distraction.

"You should get that. I don't mind." She got up and took some of the dishes back to the kitchen.

Chance pulled his phone out of his back pocket, wishing he'd remembered to put it on vibrate. It was Missy. He frowned.

Sometimes she called just to chat, but since their dad had his stroke, Chance liked to answer her straight away, just in case something was wrong. "Hey, Miss. What's up?"

"Hi, Chancey. Nothing's up. I was just wondering how you're doing. You've been grumpy since you got back from Oregon."

"I'm fine. I'm always grumpy, you know me."

She laughed. "Yeah, but I've been worried about you. I keep wondering about Hope Davenport. I saw a story about her being with some country singer and then she disappeared out of the news again."

Chance nodded. He didn't know what he could say without saying everything.

"You're going to call me crazy, but I keep hoping that she's with you, up there in Montana."

Chance laughed. He had to.

"Oh, my God! She is, isn't she?"

"Yup."

"Oh, Chance! Why didn't you tell me? I've been so worried about you."

"You worry too much. There's nothing to tell."

Hope came back out and placed the lasagna on the table.

"Hang on." Chance covered the phone with his hand. "It's my sister, Missy. I won't be a minute."

Hope smiled. "Take your time and say hi to her for me. I can put this back in the oven if you like?"

"No. I …" He could hear Missy laughing down the phone.

"Say hi back to her for me, tell I can't wait to meet her."

"Will do. I'll talk to you soon."

Missy laughed. "No, tell her now, so I can hear."

Chance chuckled. "You're a piece of work, you know?"

"I take after my big brother. Just tell her, and then you can get back to your dinner."

Chance smiled at Hope. "She says to say hi back to you and that she can't wait to meet you."

Hope smiled, and Missy chuckled down the line. "Thank you." Hope reached out for his phone, and Chance surrendered it with a sigh. There was no use resisting or thinking that he was in charge of anything when it came to these two women.

"Hello, Missy." Hope smiled at him as she spoke. "Thank you. I can't wait to meet you, too." She smiled down at him. "I'd love to. Do you think I'll be able to talk him into it?" She laughed. "I like the way you think. We'll figure it out between us. ... You too ... Okay ... Bye."

Chance was surprised to see her end the call before handing the phone back to him with a wicked smile. "I don't get to say goodbye to my sister?"

Hope laughed. "She said it was probably best for both of us if I hung up."

Chance shook his head with a rueful smile. "I'm sure it is. What's she scheming?"

"She wants us to go to Summer Lake to visit."

Chance nodded slowly. That might not be a bad idea. But then again, it might be a horrible idea. Did he really want to take Hope to the place he and Chloe had shared, to the town where they thought they'd live out their lives?

"She said if you don't like the idea, I should tell you how much your dad and Alice would like to see me again."

Chance rolled his eyes. "That's below the belt."

"She also said to remind you that she fights dirty."

He had to laugh. "She ain't kidding about that."

Hope came around the table and put her hand on his shoulder, bending down to drop a kiss on his lips. "I'm not trying to make you take me there. It's just a bit of fun. I like Missy, it's nice to be able to gang up on you with her, but I understand."

He pulled her down into his lap and kissed her deeply. Why was she so understanding? And why was it that when she did understand his doubts and his weakness, he wanted to step up and prove to her that he was better than that. When they came up for air, he smiled. "We should go. I'd like you to see the place. And she's right, Dad and Alice would love to see you again."

She grinned at him happily. "When?"

"That one's a bit tougher. Next time we meet up, we could meet there? It's much closer for you to get to from LA."

He felt like he'd said the wrong thing. A look of disappointment flashed across her face, but she covered it quickly.

~ ~ ~

Hope smiled, trying to hide her disappointment. For a moment there, she'd stupidly thought they might go to visit his family in the next few days. She needed to reel it back in. As far as Chance was concerned, this was a two-week visit, and that was all. She should be grateful that he was talking about meeting up again and taking her to see his family. She shouldn't want to rush him onto more sooner.

After they'd eaten, they sat out on the deck watching the sun go down. The sunset was amazing, the sky turning from blue to crimson to gold before the dusk finally fell. She turned to look at Chance.

He nodded. "The sky out here fascinates me; I can watch it for hours."

She smiled. "Me too, it's one of the things I love most about this place."

"And yet, you don't come here anymore?"

"I do now."

He met her gaze. "But apart from me, there's nothing for you here, is there?"

She sucked in a deep breath. It was as though he was reading the thoughts she'd had earlier. "I haven't been here, and so I don't have anything going on here. I'm sure I'd find things to do."

His brows came down. "What do you mean?"

Oh, crap. She'd been answering her own question about what she could do if she stayed here. A question that he hadn't even asked. "I mean, you make me want to be around you. If we're going to keep seeing each other in any meaningful way then we kind of need to be in the same place. I can leave LA; you can't leave here."

To her surprise, his face relaxed, and he nodded. "So, we've both been thinking about the same things again, but as usual, you're the one who's brave enough to talk about it."

She smiled. "I think dumb is a better word than brave. It's probably smarter not to bring it up till we know where we might be headed, but I can't help it. I wonder what we could do. And, honestly, if we're not going to be able to make it work, I'd rather we figure that out now."

Chance nodded sadly. "You're right, again."

"Glad you noticed." She tried to make a joke out of it, but the conversation had turned serious. "What are you thinking?" The look on his face worried her.

He sighed. "I'm trying to talk myself out of jumping to a negative conclusion."

"Good, and while you're at it, please would you talk yourself out of making any decisions that you think are best for me?"

He gave her a rueful smile. "Are you mind reading?"

"No, but I know you well enough to worry about your line of reasoning."

"Which is?"

"Obviously I don't know for certain, but I'd guess that you think since you can't leave your life here, it wouldn't be fair to ask me to leave my life in LA, so you're considering whether you should break things off with me now—and tell yourself that it's for my own good."

He nodded. "That's pretty much where I was going."

Her heart sank. "But you don't get to decide what's best for me."

"I know, and even if I did, I don't think I could go through with it."

"Why?"

"Because I don't want to lose you."

Wow! She couldn't help the smile that spread across her face. "I don't want to lose you either. So, how about instead of taking it all upon yourself to figure out what's best, you work with me? Can we be a team and figure out how we can both get what we want?"

He nodded. "I'd like that, but I don't know how to be a team."

"Neither do I, but we can figure it out as we go along. If we just keep talking to each other. Let's just be honest about everything, not make decisions by ourselves that affect the other."

"Okay. In that case, can I be honest about something that affects you?"

She nodded, wondering what was coming.

"I saw Carter today. I told you that all the brothers take a turn to host dinner each week. This week is Carter and Summer's turn. He came to ask if I wanted to bring you."

"And do you?"

He shrugged. "I don't know. Yes, part of me does. I want you to meet them; I want them to meet you. I want to show you off, I won't deny it, and part of me wants to belong in a way I never have. I want to go there as part of the family, bringing my girl with me." His smile faded. "But is it fair, is it right? How comfortable would you be?" His arm tightened around her shoulders. "And how am I going to feel in January when you're not here anymore, and every time I go to dinner with them, I remember the one time you were there?" He gave her a sad smile. "I could sit the little bear in your chair next to me, but it wouldn't be the same."

She wrapped her arms around his neck and hugged him tightly. "Thank you for telling me. I can't decide all your parts for you. I can't tell you what to do for you, but I can tell you that I'd like to go. I'd like to meet them, and I'd like to feel like a part of your life, your girl, even if it doesn't work out for us in the long run." She smiled. "Like all the tourists who never get to come back to Yellowstone again the rest of their lives, at least we'll have the bear."

He chuckled. "It's better to have loved and lost, then? Is that what you're saying?"

"I am, but I can only say that for me. I don't know if you can feel the same way. You've already loved and lost."

"I have, and for all it's cost me over the years, I wouldn't change it. I wouldn't give up the short time that Chloe and I had together just to avoid all the pain I've lived afterward."

Hope nodded. She mustn't let herself get carried away; he wasn't really talking about loving her. Was he?

Chapter Thirteen

When Chance rode back into the yard after work on Thursday, he was a little irritated to see Mason and Beau standing outside the barn talking. He didn't want to hang around wasting time with them. Hope had come down to the cabin to meet him so they could go to Carter and Summer's place together.

Beau smiled at him when he slid down from Rio. "Is Maverick still out? Seems he's been lame longer than I was."

"He's fine again now. I just want to ease him back in. I'm going to take him out mornings next week, start him out on half days."

Beau nodded. "It's a good thing you've got Rio as a backup."

Mason pursed his lips. "But we could use another backup or two. Shane's going to need Rio for ranch guests soon; the season's starting to pick up."

"I told him to just let me know when he needs him," said Chance. He'd been thinking about looking for a second horse to call his own while Maverick was out lame. His thoughts went back to Hercules, the horse he'd ridden in Oregon. He'd love to bring him out here, but he wasn't a cow horse.

Mason held up a hand. "It's all good. I need to get out of here. Gina wants to get up to Carter's place early. We're hoping to get Phoenix fed and down to sleep before we all eat."

"Good luck with that," said Beau with a grin. "You know damned well that Corinne and Summer are going to coo over her the whole time and wanting to get her up and hold her."

"Yeah. We can hope, though." Mason turned to Chance. "Speaking of Hope, are you going up the valley to pick her up?"

"No, she's waiting for me at the cabin." He tethered Rio and uncinched his saddle. "I need to take care of this guy and get home for a shower. We'll see you up there."

Mason nodded and left them to make his way up the path to the main house. Beau stayed and waited until Chance met his gaze. "Dare I ask how it's going with her?"

Chance nodded. "It's going great. She's awesome."

"I'm happy for you. Is it ... serious?"

Chance shrugged. "We'd both like it to be, but there's so much standing in the way of that."

"Like what?"

Chance let out a short laugh. "Like where we both live, our very different backgrounds, her dad, my past ... shall I go on?"

Beau chuckled. "No need. I think I get the gist of it, but it sounds to me like all those things can be overcome. Except maybe one."

Chance raised an eyebrow, wondering which one.

Beau sighed. "Where you live doesn't matter so much, if what you want most is to be together. Your backgrounds don't matter to the two of you, so whatever anyone else thinks doesn't matter. Her dad could be a big obstacle, but rich girls have run off with country boys since time began. He's an obstacle, but not an insurmountable one. The only thing that can stop the two of you is your past."

Chance blew out a sigh. He knew it was true.

Beau nodded. "But it'll only stop you if you want it to. It's your choice. Just remember that when the going gets tough, always remember that you get to decide. And I'm going to say this, and then run."

Chance smiled. "What?"

"Chloe would want you to be happy. She loved you. Don't make her your excuse not to be happy, don't blame her."

Chance closed his eyes and swallowed down the anger that surged up. "I would never blame her! It's not her fault she died!"

Beau held up a hand and backed away. "Like I told you, I need to run. I'll see you at Carter's in a little while. But think it over. Hate me for the words if you want to, but give them some thought anyway." He turned around and made his way down the new path behind the barn that led to the house he'd built down by the creek.

Once he'd gone, Chance blew out a big sigh, making Rio turn around to look at him. "It's okay, old fella." Chance rubbed his nose.

Once he'd finished brushing down Rio and turned him out, Chance made his way to the cabin. He was relieved when he saw the Land Rover parked around the side. He'd been worried when it wasn't parked out front. He walked by it, going straight to the back porch, which seemed to be Hope's favorite place to hang out. She was sitting there looking more beautiful than ever in a pair of faded jeans and a pink shirt. She smiled when she saw him.

"Hey, honey. I'm home."

She laughed. "Not for long. We're going to have to leave soon, if you don't want to be late."

Chance raised an eyebrow. She seemed on edge. Was she mad at him for being later than he said he'd be? "Yeah, I'm sorry. I ran into Mason and Beau at the barn while I was taking care of Rio."

She shook her head. "I'm not worried about that. I'm worried about being late." She was turning her bracelet around and around on her wrist.

Realization dawned, and Chance had to smile. "You're nervous?"

She hung her head and peeked up at him from under her eyebrows. "Yes."

He laughed and went to squat down in front of her. He titled her chin with his thumb, forcing her to look him in the eye. "The mighty Hope Davenport is nervous?"

She rolled her eyes. "There's nothing mighty about me. I'm a coward when it comes to meeting people. Especially important people."

He laughed. "We're talking about the Remingtons; they're my brothers in all but blood."

She nodded, her eyes wide. "Exactly! And that's what makes them so important. What if they don't like me?"

He laughed. "They're going to love you. You've already met Shane; he thinks you're awesome, the others will, too. And the girls are great."

"I'm sure they are, but they're all friends, they all know each other. I'm this intruder in their midst."

He took hold of her hand and gave it a squeeze. "They're not like that. They'll welcome you with open arms. They'll all go out of their way to make you feel comfortable. Trust me?"

"I have to."

He sighed. "No, you don't. I can call Carter and tell them we can't make it."

She shook her head rapidly. "No! You can't do that. I really do want to meet them. I'm just being silly."

Chance nodded though he tried to soften it with a smile. "It'll be fine. I need to jump in the shower if we're not going to be late, but I promise you, you'll enjoy it."

When he was ready, they got in the truck. At the top of the driveway, he stopped before turning out onto East River Road. "I wouldn't take you if I didn't think you'd enjoy yourself. If I didn't think you'd like them, or they'd like you. But I need you to know, that you're my number one priority. If you want to leave, we'll leave. You need to give me some kind of signal to come rescue you."

She reached across and took hold of his hand. "Thank you. I know I'm being silly. I'm sure they're awesome, but knowing that you've got my back means more than you know. I haven't felt like anyone's had my back my whole life. Well, except Oscar."

"In that case I like him," said Chance with a smile. "Playboy or deviant genius, or whatever he is, I don't care. If he's got your back, then he's all right in my book."

Hope smiled. "I'll remind you of that when the tables are turned, and you're about to meet him for the first time."

"Fair enough."

~ ~ ~

When Chance pulled up in front of the house, Hope looked around and nodded appreciatively. "This is beautiful."

Chance laughed. "Don't sound so surprised. They don't all live in wooden shacks like I do."

She made a face at him. "I love your cabin."

"So do I, but my point is, you shouldn't be so surprised. You know that Carter's wife is Summer Breese, the big country singer."

"I do. I should've expected a nice place."

"Right. And when we go to Shane and Cassidy's, her place would put Oscar's to shame."

"Oh!" she couldn't help sounding surprised.

Chance shook his head at her. "Yeah. She's a big-time artist. I thought you might know her. She was based in California for years."

"Well, considering I only know her as Cassidy, what's her last name? I just thought of Cassidy Remington."

"That's her name now, but she was Cassidy Lane."

"Oh!" Hope started to laugh. "Are you boys going out rounding up famous, talented women and bringing them all back here to Paradise Valley? Cassidy Lane is amazing. She's hugely talented. Just wait till Reid hears about her. He'll be coming up to visit I'm sure."

Chance shook his head. "There's no roundup going on. Cassidy and Summer both came here of their own accord and met Shane and Carter when they did." He smiled and cupped his hand around the back of her neck, drawing her closer for a kiss that left her breathless. When he lifted his head, he smiled. "Now you, you're a different matter. I guess you could say I rustled you up in Oregon and brought you back here."

She laughed. "No. I came here of my own accord, too." She reached up and touched his cheek. "Because I wanted to."

He smiled and brushed a strand of hair away from her face. "I hope you'll want to stay."

At that moment, the front door burst open and Shane came out on the front steps waving at them. "Come on in you guys!"

Chance rolled his eyes at her. "Moment destroyed, huh?"

She chuckled. "Maybe we can re-create it later?"

"I hope so. Come on, let's go do this, and don't forget, I've got your back. If you need rescuing scratch your ear or something and I'll come get you."

She squeezed his hand before opening the truck door. "Thanks, Chancey bear, you're the sweetest." She had to laugh at the thunderous look he gave her as he climbed out of the truck. "Hi Shane," she called before Chance could come around to join her. "Sorry, we're a little late."

"No, problem. You're here now. I just thought it was silly to have everyone peeking out the window at the two of you sitting there when we could get you to come inside and interrogate you as well as look!"

A woman with long blonde hair appeared behind him and swatted the back of his head. "Don't, asshole. You'll scare her away."

She turned and smiled warmly at Hope. "Ignore him, he means well." She offered her hand. "I'm Cassidy Remington, and I'm so pleased to finally meet you."

Hope shook with her. "It's a pleasure to meet you, too. I love your work. I didn't realize you were Cassidy Lane until Chance told me just now."

"Thank you."

She turned as someone else came out the door behind her. Hope had no problem recognizing Summer Breese. She'd seen her in so many music videos. She was so petite and so beautiful; the only thing that didn't look familiar about her was the baby bump. Hope would guess she was about six months pregnant. She came forward and hugged Hope. "Hi, I'm Summer. It's lovely to meet you. Come on in." She scowled at Cassidy. "We don't need to keep you standing out here on the porch." She slipped her arm through Hope's and led her into the kitchen. "Gina's putting the baby down and Beau and Corinne have taken Ruby down by the river to see the baby ducks. They'll all be back in a few minutes. Can I get you something to drink?"

"Please, I'll take whatever's on offer."

"We've got all kinds of wine," said a deep voice behind her. She turned to see a guy she assumed must be Carter since everyone else was accounted for. He looked like a body builder, big and buff, yet he immediately struck her as a gentle giant. He had such kind eyes and a calm manner about him.

"In that case, I'd love something red."

Carter smiled. "They're all the same to me. If you want to know what will go with dinner, you might want to wait for Beau; he's the expert."

She smiled. "I'll take a glass of whatever's open, thanks."

Carter smiled and poured her a glass from a bottle that looked like it came from the same winery as the Cab Franc she and Chance liked. "Do you want a glass?" he asked Chance, who was hovering by her elbow.

"I could use an ice-cold beer," he said with a grin.

"Coming right up."

Summer smiled at them. "I hope you don't have allergies, or anything, Hope? I avoided nuts and all the obvious ones, just in case."

"No, I'm pretty robust," said Hope with a smile. She hated to think of them going to any extra effort just for her.

"Good," said Shane who'd come into the kitchen behind them. "You won't last too long around here if you're not. Especially with this guy." He slapped Chance on the back.

Summer gave Shane a worried look, but Hope was grateful to him for trying to break the ice. She smiled at him. "I'm not worried about keeping up with him," she said with a smile. "He was worried at first that I might be a pampered princess, but I'm not. I guess the family name gives me a reputation that goes before me." She smiled at Summer and then Cassidy. "You both know how that goes, but I didn't even earn mine. It just comes with being a Davenport."

Cassidy grinned at her. "We're going to do just fine you and me. This one," she slapped Shane's ass, "likes to call me princess, but just because we're classy ladies, doesn't mean we can't hold our own, does it?"

Hope grinned. "Exactly."

Shane looked at Chance. "Oh dear, you have no idea what you're in for, if she's anything like Cassidy."

Chance slid his arm around Hope's shoulders. "I think I do."

Summer caught Hope's eye and smiled, and at that moment, Hope knew she would fit in with them all. For the first time since she was a little girl, she felt like she belonged in this place with these people.

A dark-haired woman came into the kitchen from the hallway. "We finally got her down ... oh, hi Chance." She smiled. "Nice to see you, Hope. I'm Gina."

Hope felt drawn to Gina. More so than the others. There was something about her that felt familiar. "It's so nice to meet you."

Gina smiled. "We've met before, but you won't remember that."

"We have?"

"Yeah. When we were kids. My dad used to lease a couple of hayfields from your dad. I used to come over with him at haying. We played a couple of times in the barn."

Hope's hand flew up to cover her mouth! "That was you? Oh,
my God! You were the only friend I had as kid up there. Gina!
I remember now. You brought me a kitten, and my dad
wouldn't let me keep it!"

Gina smiled. "Yeah, sorry, I got us both in trouble with that
one. My dad gave me hell when we got home. I'd smuggled
the kitten in the truck on the way over to you. I knew he
wouldn't let me bring it for you, but I thought it'd make you
happy."

Hope had to blink rapidly; she didn't want to cry. Not now,
not with all of them watching her, but she remembered Gina
vividly now. It was one of the many memories of her
childhood that she'd locked away. The little girl with the dark
hair who used to come over sometimes when her father came
to work the fields. Hope would slip out to see her, and they'd
play in the meadow down by the creek. Gina was so practical,
so down to earth, so different from Hope. Hope had begged
to be allowed to go and play at Gina's house, but her father
wouldn't hear of it. Now, Gina stepped forward and hugged
her and Hope clung to her, grateful for the chance to hide her
face for a moment while she regained her composure.

"Come on," said Cassidy. "It's getting a bit crowded in here.
Let's take it out on the deck and give Summer some room."
She herded Shane, Carter, and Chance out of the kitchen.

Chance put a hand on Hope's shoulder before he'd leave. She
looked up and smiled at him. "I'm okay. I'll be with you in a
minute."

Gina touched his shoulder. "I'll bring her back to you; we just
need our little reunion."

Another guy appeared in the kitchen doorway. He must be Mason, Gina's husband, judging by the way she shooed him away.

Hope straightened up and sucked in a deep breath before blowing it out. "Sorry. You just took me straight back, back to being that lonely little girl who only had one friend in the world, and you were it."

Gina smiled and rubbed her shoulder. "I didn't think you'd even remember. I wasn't going to mention it. I was just the kid from the ranch down the road. I was in awe of your house and your dad and all your things, but I still felt sorry for you somehow."

Hope nodded. "I always felt you were so much richer than I was."

"Not anymore though," Gina smiled brightly. "Now you've made your own friends and your own success in life. I love your line of leggings, and the yoga pants are the best."

"Thanks. Davenport Athleticwear is doing very well, but I can't take the credit for it anymore. I hired a great staff, and they do everything now. And as far as friends go, I still haven't made any. It's hard when you're a Davenport."

Cassidy leaned on the counter and gave her a skeptical look, making Hope nervous about what she was about to say. "It's not just when you're a Davenport. It's hard to make friends as a successful woman. We can all vouch for that; right, ladies?"

Gina and Summer nodded their agreement.

"But I'm happy to tell you, that you just stumbled into the midst of four amazing women, all of whom are successful in our own way, and all of us are happy to welcome you as a new friend. We were all in the same boat you are not so long ago. I didn't have any real friends, neither did you two, did you?"

Gina shook her head. "I made a grand total of two friends in the ten years I was away from here. They're both photographers like I am. They both live up in the Sierras now."

"I've never managed to make any friends," said Summer.

"Hey! You've always had me," said Cassidy with a scowl.

"I know," Summer smiled at her. "But if you remember, it was you and Autumn who made friends; then you just adopted me as the tag along little sister."

"Oh, yeah." Cassidy smiled. "Anyway, the point is," she turned back to address Hope, "you're here now. You've got a great group of friends on offer if you want us, and a truly great guy, if you can open him up."

Hope smiled. "I hope it's going to work out that way. I'd love to think we'll all be friends, but I don't know if Chance is going to able to let me into his life."

"Seems to me he's already let you into his life," said Cassidy. "And from the looks of him, I know he wants to let you into his heart. The million-dollar question is whether he can. Whether there's enough of his heart left."

Chapter Fourteen

Chance looked around at everyone. They were seated at the table, eating and talking. The conversation was as lively as it always was. Hope had answered lots of questions, but she seemed to be relaxed and enjoying herself. He didn't know what the story was between her and Gina, but they seemed to have an instant bond. Mason had noticed it too and had grinned at him when the two girls had told the story of the kitten Gina had brought Hope.

Little Ruby was taken with Hope and kept smiling at her and asking her questions.

"Do you want to come out riding with me?" she asked when the conversation lulled.

Hope smiled. "I'd love to."

Mason looked at Chance. "Haven't you taken Hope out yet?"

He shook his head. He hadn't had time. He was working all day, and in the evenings, they just had dinner and hung out, either up at Oscar's place or in the cabin.

Ruby smiled at him. "You can come come, too, Uncle Chancey."

"Thanks, sweetheart." He heard Hope stifle a giggle and scowled at her, not quite able to hide his smile.

Of course, Shane picked up on it. He smiled at Hope. "The rest of us wouldn't get away with calling him Chancey, just in case you wondered."

She laughed. "Oh, I don't know. I think it suits him; there's something sweet about the name Chancey, don't you think?"

Shane laughed, and Chance scowled at her, for real this time. "I am not sweet."

Cassidy laughed. "You keep telling yourself that. We know better, don't we girls?" They all smiled and nodded at him.

"Sorry, but you're not fooling anyone," said Gina. "You might like to make out you're a hard-hearted ..." she shot a look at Ruby, "kind of guy, but we know better."

Ruby nodded. "You're always sweet to me."

Chance rolled his eyes and looked around at the guys for help.

Beau shrugged. "Sorry, bro. I tried to keep up my asshole exterior ..."

"Language!" Corinne slapped his arm with a smile.

Beau smiled and planted a kiss on her cheek. "Sorry, love." He turned back to Chance. "But as you can see, these girls just strip us of our defenses. My guess is that Hope here will have you as whipped as the rest of us in no time. You're headed down the same path."

Ruby looked up at him with wide eyes. "Are you and Hope getting married."

He shook his head. "Not yet." Oh shit! He realized what he'd said when all eyes turned to him. He wasn't too concerned what the rest of them were thinking. He met Hope's gaze, but couldn't for the life of him figure out how she felt. She looked stunned, but he didn't know if she was happily stunned—or horrified.

Carter stepped in to help him out. He stood and smiled around at them. "What do you say we take it outside? It's still warm out there; it seems a shame to waste a nice evening indoors."

They all got up and started making their way outside. Chance went to Summer and took the plates out of her hands. "Why don't you go sit down with the girls? I'll give your man a hand in the kitchen."

She smiled at him. "Thanks, I will, but you can't hide in here too long. Hope might think you didn't mean what you just said."

Chance stared at her. Did he mean it? He shrugged. "It doesn't matter whether I meant it or not. It's not likely to happen, is it?"

"Why not?"

"Because there's too much in the way."

Summer smiled and patted his arm. "Nothing will stand in your way if it's what you both want. Carter and I proved that."

Chance nodded and watched her go out to join the other girls on the deck. Hope caught his eye and smiled. She didn't look so stunned now, but did she like the idea? Did he? Marriage?

"Are you going to help with the dishes or just stand there staring into space?" asked Carter.

Chance started clearing the table.

~ ~ ~

Hope couldn't believe how late it was by the time they got back to the cabin. After dinner, they'd all sat around the fire pit by the river, talking and laughing. She'd enjoyed herself more this evening than she had in a long time. They were such a great group of people, and they obviously cared so much about each other.

Chance turned to her as he opened the front door. "So?"

"So, what?"

He chuckled. "Did you have fun?"

"I did. That was the best time I've had in years." She smiled. "I'll go as far as to say you were right."

He laughed. "Can I get that in writing?"

She laughed with him. "No, you can't, but you can get my thanks for not letting me chicken out. You were right about the girls, too. They're not like the women I know in LA. There's no bitchiness or competitiveness between them. They're lovely."

Chance smiled. "They are. But not as lovely as you."

"Aww, thank you."

"Yeah, I know, I'm so sweet, right?"

She laughed. "I wasn't going to say that, but now that you mention it …"

He shook his head at her. "How tired are you? Do you want to go straight to bed?"

"Ooh, that sounds like an offer I can't refuse."

He rolled his eyes. "You're only after me for my body, aren't you?"

She laughed. "Not just that, but it helps."

"In that case, I'm going to make you wait."

"Oh."

"Yeah." It seemed he wasn't joking. "Can we sit out back for a while? I need to chill a bit after spending the evening with them all. Don't get me wrong, I love them, and I enjoy those dinners, but that's the most people time I do all week. I like to sit and watch the stars and relax afterward."

"Of course. I love that idea."

"Do you want a drink?"

She shook her head. "No, I've had enough for one night."

When they were sitting in the rockers on the back porch, she stole a peek over at him. He was leaning his head back looking up at the stars. He didn't look relaxed, though. He looked as though there was something on his mind. She wanted to ask, but if he was just unwinding, she didn't want to pull him out of his thoughts.

She leaned her own head back and looked up at the big star-filled sky. She loved the view of the night sky from her house in LA, but that was such a small stretch of sky compared to this. The skyline was man-made, created by the contours of the skyscrapers and the sky above them was always smoggy, never clear. The skyline here was created by the mountains, and the sky above them was a vast inky darkness through which millions of stars twinkled brightly.

Chance looked across at her. "What did you make of what I told Ruby?"

She froze. She'd been trying not to think about that at all. "I didn't know what to think."

He nodded. "Neither did I. I didn't even realize what I'd said until it was out."

"Did you mean it? Or was it just words coming out?"

He shrugged. "It's a bit early to even think about it, isn't it?"

She nodded. She knew it was, but part of her had been hoping that he did mean it, that somehow, he'd figured out that he couldn't live without her and that no matter what obstacles stood in their way, they would get married someday. "I suppose."

He sat up and met her gaze. "Early, but not crazy?"

She nodded, keeping her lips pressed together to contain the smile that wanted out. "No, not crazy."

He smiled. "It wouldn't be an easy ride with me, you know."

"I know. It wouldn't be an easy ride for you, either."

He nodded. "Yeah, but I'm the guy who doesn't need an easy ride, wouldn't know how to take one."

She nodded. "So, what are saying?"

He shrugged. "It's probably best not to say anything yet, right?"

"Yeah," she sighed. "No promises."

He shook his head. "Not yet, but a possibility? One we'd both like to consider?"

She smiled. "Definitely."

He nodded and got to his feet. "Let's go to bed."

~ ~ ~

The moonlight streamed in through the window casting her body in its gentle glow. Chance stood back to take in her beauty. He'd undressed her slowly and let her undress him, and now they stood naked. He felt like he was naked in every sense. They'd agreed that getting married was a possibility they'd like to consider. Maybe that was crazy. They'd only met a couple of months ago—and only spent a couple of weeks together. But if he was ever going to want to share his life with a woman, that woman would be Hope. That much he knew. What he didn't know was whether he'd be able to. Could he give her enough of himself? Could he let her into his heart? Was there room for her alongside Chloe's memory?

She stepped toward him and put her hands up on his shoulders. "Let's put aside all the talk about getting married, can we?"

He nodded. They didn't need the pressure; they needed to keep getting to know each other first. They needed to have fun, spend time together, learn each others ways—the good and the bad. Right now, what he needed to do was make love to her. He closed his arms around her waist and pulled her against him, loving the feel of her plump breasts against his chest. He lowered his head to kiss her and walked her back until her legs hit the bed. She sat down and ran her hands over his stomach, sending jolts of electricity tingling through him.

When her hands came down, and she closed them both around his length, he sucked in a deep breath and let his head fall back. Damn, that felt good. He balled his fists as he felt her warm breath on him, then her tongue. Oh, God! Her lips closed around him, and he dug his nails into his palms. Her head started to bob, and he closed his eyes, his hands coming up to tangle in her hair.

"Hope," he breathed. It felt so good, but he needed her to stop. He couldn't take much more.

She looked up into his eyes, and he shook his head, denying his instinct to thrust hard and urge her on.

She sat back, and he put a hand on her shoulder, laying her down. He wanted to give her the same kind of pleasure she'd just given him. Kneeling beside the bed, he spread her thighs and ran his hands up and down them. Her muscles were toned, and he loved the way they quivered under his touch. He slowly walked his fingers up her inner thighs, and when he reached the top, he gently parted her lips. Dipping his head, he caressed her with his tongue and was urged on by her little moans. He circled her nub with his thumb while he trailed his tongue over, then smiled at the sight of her hands grasping the sheets beneath her. He picked up his pace and rested two fingers at her entrance, dipping them just inside so he could feel the moment she was ready.

"Chance!" she gasped as he slipped his tongue deeper and kept up the pressure with the rhythm of his thumb against her most sensitive part. She was breathing heavily now; she was close. He thrust his fingers deep, and she screamed, her inner muscles clenching around him as he crooked his fingers and plunged them deeper and deeper with each stroke. Her muscles convulsed around his fingers as she writhed on the bed gasping his name until eventually, she lay still. He climbed on the bed to lie beside her, and she turned to him, sliding her arms up around his neck. "Wow!" She snuggled against him, but he wasn't looking to snuggle. He was nowhere near done with her yet.

He rolled her onto her back and positioned himself above her. Her eyes widened. "I don't know if I can yet."

He smiled. "You can."

He spread her legs with his knees and used his hand to guide himself into her opening. With his hand between them, he circled her clit with his thumb again, making her gasp, and letting him know that she could. He kept touching her as he slowly but surely slid inside her. This wasn't their usual frantic thrusting. The look on her face told him that this was exquisite torment, and that was how it felt to him, too. Her inner muscles were pulsating around him, more slowly now but still on the verge of another orgasm. He squeezed her clit between his finger and thumb and her arms and legs came up to wrap around him. He managed to get his hand out from between them. He didn't need it. The long, slow, drawn-out thrusts were enough to drive them both crazy. He could feel the pressure building at the base of his spine, but still, he moved slowly. Every thrust of his hips brought him closer to the edge. She started to buck her hips under him, increasing the pace and almost taking him over. He thrust deeper and harder, moving faster, matching her pace. She brought her legs up around his back and dug her fingernails into his shoulder. That was all he could take. His body tensed and found its release. She tightened around him, milking him for all he had to give as their bodies heaved together until they were spent.

He rested his head on her shoulder, and she turned to kiss his cheek.

"I love you, Hope," he murmured.

Her whole body tensed under him, but she didn't reply.

"I mean it. I've thought about it. I don't know what to do with it yet, but I think you should know. I've fallen in love with you."

She hugged him tightly. "I don't know if you should know this, but please understand, it doesn't come with any pressure or expectations. I love you, Chance."

He lifted his head and looked deep into her eyes. "You do?"

She nodded vigorously. "I do."

He rolled to the side and hugged her to him. "What are we getting ourselves into?"

"We don't have to get into anything. Not if we don't want to. You can love someone and accept that they're not going to be a part of your life."

He turned on his side to look into her eyes. "Is that how you see me?"

"I don't know yet. I don't want to, but I accept that it's a possibility. That doesn't stop me from loving you, and I'm glad that now you know I do. But if you hadn't told me, I don't think I would have told you."

He nodded. He'd never known a woman like her. She was up front and practical about things in a way not many people ever were. "I might not be as practical as you are."

"What do you mean?"

"I mean that loving you, and knowing that you love me back, it makes me want to fight for it, for us. It makes me want to find a way to make it happen. I'm not very good at accepting things I don't like. I don't want to accept that you're not going to be a part of my life."

She smiled. "The urge to fight for what you want is a good thing, but at the same time, so is being able to accept what you can't change."

"Yeah." It was true. If he'd been able to accept that Chloe was dead, that he wasn't ever going to be able to live the life he'd thought they would, how might his life have been?

She seemed to understand what he was thinking. "I know you've never accepted your loss."

"Yeah, and that kind of puts me in a tough place now."

"How so?"

"I don't want to accept that we can't be together. But, for us to be together, I have to finally accept that Chloe's gone and that I can be happy without her."

Hope reached up and touched his cheek. "That is tough." She sighed. "But we're not going to figure any of it out tonight, are we?"

"No."

She snuggled into his side. "So, we may as well sleep on it."

He dropped a kiss on her hair. He didn't know if he'd be able to sleep at all. Now that he'd told her that he loved her, now she'd said she loved him, he wanted to figure it all out at once. He wanted to slay all the dragons, overcome all the obstacles in their way, right now. He wasn't any better at patience than he was at letting go.

"If we're meant to be together, it'll all work out," said Hope.

"Maybe." Chance preferred to control his own fate. Even though life had tried to teach him that he couldn't. "Are you going back up to Oscar's place in the morning?"

"Yes, and I'm going to meet Gina for lunch."

Chance smiled. He loved the idea of the two of them becoming friends. He liked all the girls, but he'd known Gina longest. He also liked the idea that she been a little part of Hope's past here. "That's great."

She nodded sleepily. "I think so. I'll come back down here for when you finish work, if you like?"

"I could come up to Oscar's if you prefer?"

"No, I like it here better."

He smiled. He did, too.

Chapter Fifteen

Hope couldn't find a place to park anywhere near The Mint. She had to leave the Land Rover a few blocks away and walk back. It was a beautiful day. Spring would soon turn into summer; she could feel it in the air.

She was relieved when she saw Gina standing outside waiting for her. She didn't like to walk into places by herself. She always felt like there might be a photographer or reporter waiting inside to ambush her. She didn't worry about that so much up here. The press didn't seem to have found Montana on the map yet, and she was grateful for that.

Gina smiled and waved when she spotted her. "Hey, I'm so glad you could make it."

"Me too. Is the baby with Mason?"

"No, he's busy at the stud. I left Phoenix with Summer and Carter for a couple of hours. They love to have her whenever they can. I think they're practicing on her for when their baby arrives."

Hope smiled. "It must be nice, for you and the little one, to have all those aunts and uncles on hand when you need them, and soon there'll be lots of little cousins to play with, too."

Gina nodded, as she pushed the door open and held it for Hope to go inside. "We're all looking forward to that. Corinne and Beau are trying to get pregnant now."

"Ruby's not his daughter, is she?" asked Hope as they sat down in one of the booths.

"She's not his biological daughter, but he adopted her when they got married, and she calls him daddy. He really is her daddy in everything but blood."

"That's what Chance says about the guys; that they're his brothers in all but blood."

"And they are. He didn't grow up here, but he's been a part of the family since he arrived. The bond between them all just grows stronger with every year that passes."

"That must be so nice—to grow closer over the years. I've only found myself drifting further and further apart from my family as the years go by."

Gina nodded. "I can understand that. I was gone from here for ten years. I felt as though I'd lost my family and my roots. I missed my dad so much, but he wouldn't leave here, and I couldn't stay here. Other than him, the only family I'd ever had were the Remingtons, and I'd lost them too. Don't you see your cousins anymore?"

Hope shrugged. "Not really. I talk to Oscar on the phone every couple of months. I haven't talked to TJ since he left the military, and Reid, well, I never really talked to him as much as the others. He's not the kind to talk on the phone, and I never know whereabouts in the world he is. They haven't all been home for Christmas in the last few years, and that was when we used to catch up."

Gina nodded. "What do you do for Christmas?"

Hope sighed. "For a while, we all went to Uncle Johnny and Aunt Jean's. The boys all used to come home. I'd join them, Dad even came a couple of times, but I suppose everyone's moved on with their own lives, and now we all just do our own thing."

"You don't see your dad for the holidays?"

Hope shrugged. "Sometimes. We'll video chat if he's away."

Gina shook her head sadly. "So, you've got no one?"

Hope laughed. "Don't look so sorry for me. I'm not the poor little rich girl anymore. I have ..." She was going to say she had friends, but that wasn't entirely true. "I know people."

Gina gave her a skeptical look. "But no one means much to you, do they? No one's got your back in life."

"Chance does." Hope smiled, remembering how he'd told her that last night and how much it meant to her.

Gina smiled back. "He's a great guy. You've made him happier than I've ever seen him."

"He makes me happy, too."

"I can see that. Do you think the two of you are going to make it? I'd love to think that you will, and that, come Christmas, you'll have all of us as your family. That you and Chance will be another aunt and uncle to Phoenix, and maybe even provide her with some more cousins."

Hope closed her eyes for a moment and was pleased when the server came to take their order.

Once he'd gone, Gina smiled. "Sorry, I got carried away there."

"No more carried away than I've been getting," admitted Hope. "I'd love to think all of that might be possible, but I'm not sure that it will be."

"Chance has come a long way in a short time since he met you."

"I believe that, but I don't know if he's got enough room left in his heart to be able to be happy with me. And besides, even if he can get past his demons, I'm not sure I can get past my dad."

"He doesn't like Chance?"

"He's never met him, but he doesn't like the idea of him."

"I'm sure he'll change his mind when he does meet him."

Hope shrugged.

"You don't plan to introduce him?"

"I'm not looking forward to it."

Gina smiled. "I find that the things you aren't looking forward to are the ones you should do straight away. Get them over with."

"I know, and I'm usually pretty good about that. I seem to screw up when it comes to Chance though. I put things off because I'm scared they won't work out the way I want them to."

Gina nodded. "I think we all do that when it comes to the things that are most important to us."

Hope thought about it. "You're right; I should get it over with. If Dad still has a problem with Chance after he meets him, then I'm going to need time to work on him. The sooner I get started on that the better, right?"

Gina grinned. "I'd say so."

The server came back with their food, and they started to eat. Gina stopped with her fork poised in midair. "What would you do if you stayed here?"

Hope shrugged. "That's another big obstacle. My business is in LA, and that's where it needs to be. I can live here and leave my staff to run it. They're better at it than I am, anyway. But," she blew out a sigh, "what could I do here?"

Gina shook her head. "I don't know. I had a hard time believing that I'd be able to make enough to get by here. If it weren't for Cassidy, I'm still not sure I'd be able to."

"Well, I don't paint, I don't take photographs, I couldn't run a guest ranch like Corinne does. I sure as hell can't sing."

Gina laughed. "Summer doesn't sing anymore either. She's just waiting for the baby to arrive and then she'll be a full-time mom." She raised an eyebrow.

Hope shook her head rapidly. "Yes, I'd love to have kids, but no I couldn't be a full-time stay-at-home mom. Don't get me wrong, I admire people who can do that, but I'm not one of them. I need to be doing something for myself as well."

Gina smiled. "I know that feeling. Phoenix is my whole world, but at the same time, she's a part of my world. I want her to grow up knowing that she can do anything she wants to, that she doesn't have to choose, she can do it all."

Hope nodded her agreement. "I'm not sure I'll ever have children, but even if I do, I'll still need a career, and I don't see what kind of career I could have here."

Gina shook her head. "I wish I had some bright ideas for you, but I don't. I'll give it some thought. In the meantime, I think you should talk to your dad. I think you should let him know how important Chance is to you."

"Yeah."

"You don't sound convinced."

"Another reason I've been putting off talking to my dad about Chance is that I don't want to do it if Chance and I aren't going to make it anyway."

Gina pursed her lips. "I can understand that, but, at some point, you've got to come down from the fence and go for it. You can't hang back and wait to see if it's going to be possible. You need to move forward and fight to make it possible."

"I know, but what if I win my dad over and Chance decides he doesn't love me enough?"

Gina grinned.

"What?"

"He's already told you he loves you?"

Hope nodded. "But please don't tell him I told you? We've both said it, but we're not ready to face it yet."

"I won't say a word, but it sounds to me like you both already know that you're going to be together, you know where you're going, just not how you're going to get there."

"I'd like to think you're right."

"I am, and on your wedding day I'll remind you of this conversation."

Hope smiled. "That's one I told you so that I'd be more than happy to hear."

After lunch, Gina walked her back to the Land Rover and gave her a hug. "I hope I'll see you again before you leave?"

"Me too. Can I call you?"

"Any time. If you and Chance want to come over for dinner one night, just let me know. Mason would love to have you. We talked about inviting you, but we haven't wanted to take up the little time the two of you have together."

"Thanks. I think I need to get to work on figuring out how we can extend our time. It's going to be down to me to figure that out. Chance's life is what it is. He's here; his work takes up most of his time. If I want to be with him, I need to adapt to that somehow."

"And, are you okay with that?"

"I am, it's my choice to make. I'll be a lot happier with it if I can figure out what I'd do with my time here, though."

"Would you mind if I talk to Cassidy about it? She's great at ideas; she's sees possibilities and opportunities everywhere."

"Okay. I'm not coming up with anything by myself; maybe she can see something we can't."

Gina smiled. "She usually does. I'm going to pop into the gallery before I go and pick Phoenix up. I'll have a chat with her."

"Thanks."

Hope had a lot on her mind as she drove back down to Oscar's place. If she was going to make the leap, decide that she was going to do everything she could so she and Chance could be together, then she had a lot of decisions to make. The biggest one was whether she should invite her dad to meet him. Maybe she should figure out what she could do to make a life for herself here first? Her dad might be more receptive if he could see that moving here would be a good move for her personally and that it didn't depend totally on her relationship with Chance. Hell, she'd be a lot happier if she could see that, too.

When she approached Uncle Johnny's, both he and Aunt Jean were sitting out on the front porch. She stopped the Land Rover and rolled down her window. "Hi there." She knew something was amiss from the look on their faces. "What's wrong?"

"You haven't heard from your father?" asked Uncle Johnny.

Her heart began to race. "No. Is he okay?" No matter how strained their relationship might be at times, she often woke up crying after nightmares that he'd died. She dreaded that someday he'd be gone and he wouldn't know how much she loved him.

"He's fine." Uncle Johnny gave her a reassuring smile. "He's coming here."

"Here?"

Uncle Johnny nodded solemnly.

"Oh. Why?"

"His exact words were, he's concerned about his daughter running around with some cowboy. He's also concerned that your aunt and I are not doing enough to keep you in check."

Aunt Jean smiled. "In fact, we're probably a bad influence, or at least I am."

Uncle Johnny shook his head at her. "He didn't say that."

She laughed. "No, but he thinks it. He always has." She looked at Hope. "Do you think Chance is ready to face an inquisition?"

Hope blew out a sigh. "I don't know, but I guess we're about to find out. When did Dad say he'd be here?"

"Tomorrow morning."

"Wow! That soon?"

"Yes, and he said he's prepared to take you home with him if he doesn't like what he finds."

Hope let out a bitter laugh. "Which of his houses is he calling home these days? The one in the Caymans? The only place I've ever called home was our house here, and he took me away from it when I needed it most. He has no right to say what I do or where I will call home."

Uncle Johnny looked shocked by her outburst, but Aunt Jean smiled kindly. "You're bound to be upset, Hopey, but you should calm down before you talk to him. Prepare your argument with logic that he can't deny."

Hope nodded.

"Do you want to come in for a while?" asked Uncle Johnny. "Maybe we can plan your defense?"

"Or your line of attack?" suggested Aunt Jean.

Hope checked the clock on the dash. It was only two-thirty. Chance wouldn't be finished with work till at least six. She'd do better to hang out with them than to sit at Oscar's place fuming over her father's imminent arrival. She nodded and got out of the truck.

~ ~ ~

Chance loved coming home to the cabin and finding Hope sitting out on the back porch waiting for him. It made him feel like this was his life, and that his life was complete. He smiled at the sight of her. She smiled back, but something was wrong. He could tell straight away.

"What is it?"

She shook her head and blew out a sigh. "Is it that obvious? I haven't even said hello yet."

"Yeah, but there's something wrong. I can tell by that little line on your forehead, and by the way, the corners of your mouth turn down the tiniest bit."

She smiled. "That better?"

"Kind of, your mouth is smiling, but your eyes aren't. Are you going to tell me?"

"Yeah. My dad's coming."

"Oh. He knows you're here then?"

She nodded.

"And he knows you're with me?"

She nodded again.

Chance closed his eyes and pressed his lips together. "Last night I told you that I want to fight against all the obstacles in our way." He shook his head. "I don't want to fight your dad. I don't want to come between the two of you."

She met his gaze. "What are you saying?"

He held up a hand. "I'm not backing out. I'm just saying I don't know how to handle this."

"Well, you said you've got my back, right?"

"Yep."

"And you're not going to try to make my decisions for me?"

"No. I'm not, but I don't want to cause friction between the two of you."

"You won't. If there's any friction, it will caused by him not having my back and by trying to make my decisions for me. I want him to respect me, to respect what I want, and I want him to accept that I want to be with you, that I want to live here."

"You do?"

She nodded. "Yes. I need to find something I can do with my life here. I can't just be a porch ornament in your life."

He smiled at the way she put it, but he understood what she meant. "What about your business, though?"

She shrugged. "There are a lot of details to be worked out and decisions to be made, but that'll all happen with time. The big decision is made. I'm moving here."

Chance looked at her for a long moment. He didn't want her to rush into this just to defy her father. He didn't want to be responsible for her giving up the life she had. Especially when he didn't know what kind of life she could have here.

"Unless you don't want me to?"

"I do! It's not that."

"What then?"

"I want you to do what's best for you."

She got up and came to him. Sliding her arms around his waist, she looked up into his eyes. "As far as I'm concerned, you're what's best for me."

He lowered his mouth to hers. Her plump, pink lips were so soft against his. The way she kissed him back told him she wanted him. This wasn't about defying her father; it was about being with him. Her kiss told him that.

When he lifted his head, he nodded. "So, how are we going to approach it? What do you want me to do?"

"How do you feel about meeting him?"

"Determined, nervous, a whole mix of emotions. I'd love to think he'll like me, but I doubt he will. I understand where he's coming from—he wants to protect his daughter. I can relate to that. He perceives me as a possible threat. At the very least, he thinks I'm not good enough for you. I'd like to prove him wrong, but I don't know if he'll give me the opportunity to do so. If he's determined not to like me, if he doesn't want me to be in your life, then we're going to have a real problem."

She nodded. "We are, but as far as I'm concerned, it will be his problem. Not ours. He has to accept that I make my own decisions, and he can like it or lump it."

Chance chuckled. "I haven't heard that expression in years."

She smiled. "He used to say that all the time to me when I was little. It's helped me learn that sometimes we just have to accept what we can't change." She sighed.

"What?"

"I just know he'll think he can change my mind."

"Maybe he will."

She frowned at him. "No way."

"If you say so, but I don't want this to make you lose sight of things."

"What things?"

"Before you knew he was coming, we were going to just take it as it comes, we were aiming for a possibility, but no more than that. I don't want you to get so busy fighting your dad that you forget to decide if you really want us. When someone tells you you can't have something, you end up fighting to get it, just out of defiance. You forget to question whether you really wanted it in the first place."

She smiled. "You're right, but this is different. I do want you, I want us, but I'm not going to rush us, just because he's trying to put a stop to it."

"Is that what he's doing?"

She shrugged. "Not yet, but I know that's what he will do if we can't win him over."

"Okay, I'd better do my best to win him over then, huh? When does he arrive?"

"Tomorrow morning."

"Should I get the guys to cover for me and take the day off?"

"No. I'll see him by myself during the day, then we can figure out if we're all going to have dinner together or something."

Chapter Sixteen

Hope sat on the deck at Oscar's place. Her dad should be here any time now. She could have gone to the airport to meet him, but she didn't want to. She felt like that would be going running just because he'd snapped his fingers. He'd be staying up at the house. She didn't want to go there. It wasn't her home anymore. She was more comfortable here, in her cousin's house. Being here felt like she had her own territory; he could come into it. She wasn't going to sit and wait for him in a house full of childhood memories. She wouldn't do it. She blew out a sigh. She needed to calm down before he arrived. She was angry with him. Angry that he felt he had the right to dictate what she did with her life and angry that he hadn't even called her. He'd talked to Uncle Johnny and now just expected her to be there waiting for him when he arrived. She sighed again. She really needed to calm down.

Her heart began to race in her chest when she heard a vehicle coming down the lane. This was it. He was here. She watched as the SUV pulled up out front. Her father climbed out of the passenger seat. He rarely drove himself anywhere anymore. His bodyguard did all the driving.

He looked up at her, and her frosty attitude melted a little when he smiled. "Hey, Hopey."

"Dad!" She ran down the steps to meet him and wrapped him in a hug. She couldn't help it. She loved him despite everything.

He hugged her to him for an all too brief moment, then stepped back and held her at arm's-length. "You look well. Very well. You're healthier and happier than the last time I saw you aren't you?"

"I am, and I think you know why."

His smiled disappeared in an instant. "Are we going to get straight into it?"

She shrugged. "I thought that was what you came for? It's not like you normally just drop in to see me, is it?"

"No, it isn't. I try to let you get on with your life."

"I wish you would."

He fixed her with a hard glare. "I do. Mostly. Until you get too far off track, then I feel the need to offer a little parental guidance—because I love you, not because I'm trying to control you or your life."

Hope drew in a deep breath and let it out slowly. There was no point getting angry. It wouldn't help anything; it'd only make matters worse. "I know you mean well, I really do. I just hope you've come with an open mind."

"I have. I won't deny that I have some major concerns, but I'm prepared to keep an open mind, and to listen to you—and to him if you'll let me. If he's up to it."

"He's up to it. He wanted to be here to greet you when you arrived. Don't think he's trying to hide from you, because he isn't. I was the one who said he should wait. I wanted to talk to you by myself first."

Her dad nodded. "That's good to know—about both of you."

"What do you mean?"

"I mean I'm glad to hear he's got the balls to want to meet me and glad to hear that you wanted to talk to me alone first." He

smiled gently. "It makes me think that maybe there's still a
chance for you and me. That you're not just going to cast me
aside because of him."

"No! My goodness, no, Dad. I always wanted there to be a you
and me. I wanted to be able to come to you first—about
boyfriends and everything else, but you … you didn't have
room for me, or time for me, or you were trying to make me
stand on my own two feet. I never felt I could."

He closed his eyes for a moment. "I've always been here for
you, Hopey. I just don't know how to be… I don't know how
to …"

Hope was stunned by the pain that shone in his eyes. At that
moment, she understood something about him that she never
had before. He and Chance were the same kind of animal.
"You want to love me, but you don't know how to let
yourself?"

He shook his head. "I do love you. I don't know how to show
you." He visibly pulled himself together. "Are you going to
invite me in?"

She nodded and led him up the steps to the front door.

"Why didn't you stay at the house?" he asked as he followed
her through to the kitchen.

She shrugged. "I can't bring myself to stay there. It hurts too
much." As she said it, she was getting at him, letting him know
that she hadn't forgiven him for taking her away from that
house after her mom died. His response knocked her for six.

"It hurts me, too, but I can't come here and not stay there.
That's why I come so rarely. That place is all about your mom.
It's a mausoleum to the life we lost, the life I've never stopped
wanting back."

Hope had to turn away and wipe her eyes. He really was just
like Chance. She understood so much more about him now
than she had before. If she tried to understand him in the

same way she understood Chance, everything looked so different.

"I'm sorry. I've been on the go for the last several days. I'm sleep deprived, and, apparently, a little emotional. Forgive me?"

She turned around and let the tears roll down her cheeks. "I forgive you, Daddy. Can you forgive me? I never understood how it must feel for you. All I could see was my own pain and how you made it worse. I think I understand you now. I'm sorry."

He wrapped his arms around her and hugged her to his chest. "You were just a little girl. I didn't know what to do. I couldn't see past my own pain. I'm sorry."

She sobbed into his chest and hugged him back, feeling closer to him than she had since she was twelve years old. "I love you."

"I love you, Hopey."

They stood that way for a long time. This couldn't be further from the meeting she'd expected to have with him.

Eventually, he straightened up and wiped his eyes. "I'm still concerned about this cowboy."

She nodded. "His name is Chance. I know you're concerned, that's why I want you to meet him. Before I heard you were coming here, I was trying to figure out a time I could bring him to meet you."

"You were?"

She nodded. "He's important to me. I need you to understand that."

"What's so special about him? You've never wanted me to meet any of the others."

"None of the others mattered much. Chance does."

"What do you see in him?"

She smiled. "He's a decent, honorable man. He reminds me a lot of you."

Her father's eyes widened. "How?"

"He has high standards; he doesn't have much faith in people." She drew in a deep breath before she said what she'd only just understood herself. "He's wasted half his life mourning the woman he loved."

He stared at her for a long moment.

She wanted to say something to break the silence, but she forced herself not to. She wanted him to think about her words and what they meant before he responded.

Eventually, he nodded. "And you find that an admirable trait in him?"

"I respect it, both in him and in you, but I also see the damage it's done. To both of you." She smiled. "I'd like to think I can be the catalyst that helps you both rejoin the living."

He frowned.

"At first, Chance didn't feel as though he should allow himself to get close to me because that would mean he'd have to let go of Chloe. I told him he doesn't need to let go of her; she's a part of him." She held his gaze. "Just like Mom is a part of you and a part of me. We don't have to shut ourselves down to feeling anything for anyone else. Mom's inside us, no matter where we go and no matter who we allow ourselves to love. Mom will always be a part of us."

Her dad wiped his eyes and nodded slowly. "So, this isn't going to be a case of me buying off an undesirable who's got his hooks into you?"

She let out a bitter little laugh. "Do you really think I'm that stupid?"

He sighed. "No, I suppose I was just hoping it could be that simple. When do I get to meet him?"

"I told him I'd call him about coming up here for dinner this evening."

"Do I get you to myself until then?"

She smiled. "I'd love that. What would you like to do?"

His lower lip trembled. "Would you come up to the house with me?"

She grasped his hand tightly. "Yes. Maybe it's time we went in there together."

~ ~ ~

Chance paced the cabin after his shower. He was nervous! Dammit. He hated feeling this way. He shouldn't care what some rich guy thought about him. But he did. He cared because that guy was Hope's father. No matter what she'd said about him having to like it or lump it, it wasn't that simple. It couldn't be. He was her father, and Chance held that bond sacred—even if Hope claimed not to.

She'd asked him to come up to Oscar's place at seven. They were going to have dinner with her dad—just the three of them. Before he'd left her this morning, they'd discussed the possibility of having Uncle Johnny and Aunt Jean join them. It might be better to have them in his corner. Hope had said she'd see how things were with her dad before she decided. She'd decided against asking them, and Chance could only hope that was a good sign—that they didn't need them there to referee or to temper her father's fury. Maybe she just didn't want them to witness his fury?

One thing Chance knew was that he had to keep his own temper firmly in check. He could not—would not—allow himself to get angry. He found it hard not to defend himself if someone attacked him verbally, but he had to keep himself on a tight leash. There were plenty of things he was angry at Seymour Davenport for, but he couldn't air them. He had to respect the guy. He was Hope's father, no matter what Chance thought of his fathering abilities or about the harm he'd done to his daughter ... He stopped and gave himself a shake. Just remembering what he shouldn't get wound up about was getting him wound up!

He checked the clock on the wall. He should go. He'd still be early if he went now, but he'd rather get closer and stop in a pull out to kill some time than having to hang around here any longer.

~ ~ ~

Hope put a bowl of nuts down on the table in front of her dad with a smile. They were sitting out on the deck having a drink before dinner. "Do you think you can be as nice to Chance as you've been to me today?" They'd spent an emotional afternoon up at the house. She felt exhausted now, and she knew her dad did, too—emotionally, if not physically. They'd talked about her mom and shared memories of the life they'd had when they lived there. They'd both shed a lot of tears, but she felt better for it.

He made a face, that looked like it might be an attempt at a smile, but didn't quite make it. "I can't be as nice to him. He's not my daughter. He's a threat ..."

"Oh, Dad!" She'd thought they'd made some progress today, but apparently not.

He held up a hand. "I should have put that differently. This isn't about him, in particular. I don't mean Chance Malone is a threat. I mean any father sees the man his daughter has fallen in love with as a threat."

Hope stared at him open-mouthed.

"What?"

"You just said two things, that I hadn't told you."

He frowned.

"I never told you his last name was Malone, and I haven't said I love him."

This time his smile was more genuine. "Even I can see you love him; there's no point denying that. And as for knowing his last name, you're not going to pretend to be surprised that I had him checked out, are you?"

She shook her head. "No. I mean you knew about his past, about the time he spent in prison."

His face tightened. "And you wonder why I see him as a threat? You wonder why I'm not thrilled by the thought of you giving up your whole life to be here with him?"

"It's not like that. It's ..." She stopped, and they both turned at the sound of a vehicle approaching. Chance's big black pickup appeared and came to a stop in front of the house. "Please, Dad. I understand you have your reservations, but please keep an open mind? Assess the man you meet tonight—don't judge the man you've already decided he is?"

He nodded slowly. "I'll try."

Hope walked around the deck on the side of the house and waved at Chance. "Come on up this way; we're making the most of the sun while it lasts."

Chance bounded up the stairs and swiped his hat off when he reached her. He looked gorgeous, even more so than usual. He was freshly showered and shaved, and he smelled wonderful. He dropped a kiss on her cheek and handed her a bottle of wine. "I brought this." She could tell he was nervous. She wanted to hug him, to reassure him, but she knew that would just make him more uncomfortable with her dad watching them.

She took hold of his hand and squeezed it as she led him over to the table. Her dad got to his feet, and she was relieved to see that he attempted a friendly smile. She knew him well enough to recognize the tension around his mouth, but, hopefully, Chance wouldn't notice. "I want you to meet the other most important man in my life, my dad, Seymour Davenport. Dad, this is Chance Malone."

Chance stepped forward and offered his hand. "It's an honor to meet you, sir."

For a moment, Hope thought her dad wasn't going to shake with him. He gave Chance a long appraising look before he took his outstretched hand with a nod. "I won't lie. I can't say it's a pleasure."

Hope's heart sank, but Chance nodded. "Thank you. I do better with honesty than fake niceties."

She was relieved when her dad smiled. "Good, then we've already found one thing we have in common. I can honestly say that I'm glad to meet you. You're important to my daughter, and whether or not I like what I find, I want to get to know you."

"Likewise."

Hope had to hide a smile; she thought she even saw the shadow of a smile on her dad's face. He might have said he did better with honesty than fake niceties, but that was only when he was the one being honest. He wasn't used to people being honest with him.

"Okay, now that the worst is over, can I get you both a drink? Dinner's going to be a little while yet."

Chance eyed her dad's gin and tonic and smiled. "I'd love a cold beer, thanks."

Hope nodded. She hoped Chance wasn't going to go all out to prove to her dad just how different they were. "Can I get you a fresh one, Dad?" she asked, picking up his empty glass.

He took her by surprise when he replied, "I'll have a cold beer, too, thanks." He smiled at Chance.

Hope shook her head as she went inside. It was as if the two of them were playing some kind of mental chess game, each trying to catch the other off guard with an unexpected maneuver. She deliberately took her time rinsing her dad's glass and pouring herself a stiff one. She wanted to leave them alone together long enough to have to talk to each other, but not long enough that they might get into an argument.

She pulled the chicken thighs out of the oven to check on them. Another ten minutes and they'd be done. They were her father's favorite, or at least they used to be, baked with shallots, olives and cherry tomatoes in just enough olive oil to stop them from drying out. She set her drink on a tray, then smiled to herself as she took two bottles of beer from the fridge. She wasn't going to bring glasses out for them. Chance drank straight from the bottle; she wondered if her father would, too.

She stopped when she reached the French doors that led back out to the deck. There was no icy standoff that she'd been half fearing. Chance and her dad were standing side by side, leaning on the rail of the deck. Chance was pointing down the valley, saying something she couldn't hear. Her dad had a hand on Chance's shoulder and looked as though he was actually listening. She had to swallow the lump that rose in her throat and blink away tears at the sight of them—it made her so happy, but she mustn't get carried away. It was just a moment in time, not the resolution of all her problems.

Chapter Seventeen

The next morning, Chance got Rio ready and tethered him to the rail in the yard before going back to the barn to bring Maverick out. He still couldn't quite believe he was doing this. Last night had gone much better than he'd dared imagine. Hope's father hadn't turned out to be the snooty, closed-off man Chance had expected. He actually liked the guy, which had surprised the hell out of him. He was sharp, which shouldn't have surprised him. He'd have to be sharp to have amassed the fortune he had. More than that even, Chance felt a kinship with him that he hadn't expected to. He'd gone into last night seeing the two of them as competitors, rivals for Hope's affection, in a battle Chance had thought he couldn't win, that he wouldn't want to win because Seymour—as he'd told Chance to call him—was her dad. As the evening had gone on, he'd understood that Seymour was weighing him up, testing him, not because he wanted to run him off, but because he wanted to assess whether Chance was worthy of being his teammate, whether between the two of them they could ensure Hope's happiness and well-being. He'd gained a lot of respect for the guy during dinner. Afterward, the three of them had sat outside again. Seymour had talked about how much he used to love the valley and Chance's sense of kinship with him had grown when he understood why he stayed away now. He hadn't said too much about Hope's mom, but he'd given enough away to make Chance think about Chloe—about how he'd left Summer Lake after her death. He hadn't gone back for years. For the longest time, he couldn't stand to be there. The last few years had taken him back more and more—because of family. He wondered whether the same might happen for Seymour. If Hope were to move here, would that draw him back? Would it help him come to terms with his loss? He blew out a sigh. Who knew?

All he should be focusing on right now was getting Maverick ready. Seymour would be here soon. They were going to ride out together. This had been the most surprising result of their conversation last night. Seymour had asked Chance about his work, about the Remington ranch, and the cattle he ran. Chance had been surprised how knowledgeable he was, both about ranching and the valley. When he'd said he missed riding and feeling a part of the valley, Chance had offered to take him out this morning. He wanted to show him his life, wanted him to understand who he was and what he did. He also wanted to help him enjoy something he hadn't done in years—and maybe help him reconnect with this place that it seemed he used to love so much.

He turned to watch an SUV coming up the driveway, sending up a trail of dust in its wake. That was him. Chance tightened the cinch of Maverick's saddle, hoping that this was going to work out and that it hadn't been a dumb idea.

The SUV came to a stop, and Seymour climbed out of the passenger seat, making Chance wonder where the driver had been hiding last night. There'd been no sign of him. Did he sit and wait in the vehicle everywhere Seymour went? He got a grip; that wasn't the most pressing question right now as Seymour strode across the yard to greet him.

"Good morning. We've got a great day for it."

Chance nodded. The sky was blue, and the sun was already warm. "We do. It might get hot after a while, but we can come back whenever you're ready."

Seymour smiled. "I can keep up, don't worry about me."

Chance smiled. He did look to be in great shape. "You just let me know. I don't want us trying to outdo each other to the point of exhaustion."

Seymour laughed. "Fair point, but you let me know if you can't keep up, too?"

Chance laughed with him. "Okay. I've got you riding Rio; he'll take care of you."

Seymour nodded, and Chance liked him more as he went to stroke Rio's nose. "I'll try not to get in your way, Rio."

Chance untethered him and led him out to the center of the yard. "There's a mounting block if …"

Seymour gave him a stern look. "I'm not that old yet." He took the reins and mounted Rio easily as if he'd ridden all his life.

Chance nodded and went to get on Maverick. "I'm not trying to put you down, I'm just trying to look out for you," he said as he climbed into the saddle.

Seymour smiled. "I know, but I'm sure you can understand that when you judge me to be something other, something less than I am, I have to prove what I'm capable of."

Chance reined Maverick around and smiled at him. "I sure as hell can relate to that."

"So, how about we each wait to see what the other can do before we go making any more judgments?"

"Sounds good to me. Let's go." Chance headed out of the yard and up the trail that led to the western pastures. After their conversation last night, he wanted to take Seymour out to where the Remington land adjoined his own land. If he wanted to, they could ride over his property which it sounded like he hadn't done in decades.

Seymour brought Rio up alongside Maverick. He rode well. He must have spent a lot of time in the saddle at some point in his life. He looked like he belonged there. Chance smiled. "You look at home. Have you ever thought about giving it all up and coming back here to run cattle?"

Seymour didn't laugh; instead, he nodded solemnly. "You'd be surprised how many times I have thought about doing just that." He met Chance's gaze. "But you'll probably understand better than most why I haven't."

"I think I do. I didn't go back to Summer Lake for years after Chloe died."

Seymour nodded, and they rode on in silence for a while, making Chance feel he'd missed an opportunity to share something important. "I've been going back more and more lately, though."

"And why's that?"

"Family, mostly. The passing of time, partly."

"Your father and your sister are still there, aren't they?"

Yeah, and my nephew, and Chloe's sister, and a whole bunch of friends who mean a lot to me."

"Perhaps I can learn from you."

Chance didn't say anything. He's only wanted to share how he was learning to deal with his loss in a more constructive way. He hadn't meant to push Seymour anywhere.

"If Hope were here, if she lived here …" He turned in the saddle to meet Chance's gaze. "I've accepted a lot about you since I've met you. You're a better man than I thought." He pursed his lips. "Let's be honest; you're a better man than I wanted you to be."

Chance smiled, grateful that was the case and perhaps even more grateful that Seymour was prepared to admit it.

"One thing puzzles me though."

"What's that?" Chance braced himself for the reply. Seymour had used the word puzzled, but his expression looked like, whatever it was, angered him.

"If you love her, if you know her well and you understand her, how can you expect her to move here? Do you honestly see her being happy as a rancher's wife? Don't you think there's more to her than that?"

"Hell yes, I do! I don't like the idea of her giving up her life any more than you do."

"But you're not prepared to give up yours in order to be with her?"

It was a fair question. Chance knew that. "I could, I've considered it, but this isn't just what I do. It's who I am. If you were to land me in LA, I'd shrivel and die within weeks. I can't handle being in the city, any city. I can't handle the people, the traffic, the buildings. I'd make her miserable. I know that. I also know it must seem selfish of me." He nodded to himself. He hadn't needed Seymour to point out how one-sided it seemed; it'd been on his mind too. "There's something you should know."

They reached a gate, and Seymour reined Rio back to let Chance and Maverick go ahead of them and open it. After he'd closed it behind them, they rode on in silence for a little while.

"I'm waiting for you to tell me what I should know, but I'm not sure I want to hear it."

"You might like it. You need to know that Hope and I aren't as far along in our relationship as you seem to think. We know we'd like to be together, but at this point, it's only a possibility. We haven't known each other very long, and much as we feel the connection, we were thinking we should take our time. See how things develop rather than forcing them to happen."

"Until I came along?"

Chance nodded. "Yup."

"Are you saying you're not sure if she's the one for you?"

Chance met his gaze. "She's the only woman alive I will ever want to be with."

"But there's one who's no longer alive, too."

"I didn't mean that so much as I meant, I'm no more comfortable with the thought of her giving up her life to be here with me than you are."

Seymour nodded. "What if we could figure out a good life for her here?"

Chance shook his head. "If there's one thing I know, it's that we can't figure anything out for her. She has to do it herself."

Seymour laughed so heartily that Rio lunged sideways in surprise. Chance was glad to see that he stayed in the saddle with ease. "Sorry." He patted the horse's neck and looked at Chance. "The irony amused me. To think that we could both lose her by trying to work together to help her."

Chance nodded; he didn't find the prospect quite so amusing.

They rode on in silence for a while, until they came to the farthest reaches of the ranch. "The Remington land ends right over there." Chance pointed to the fence. "On the other side, you're back on your own land."

"It's been years since I've been down here." He looked at Chance. "Do you resent me, and the others like me who own large tracts of land, but don't live on it or work it?"

"No. It's not ideal, I'd like to see the whole valley ranched and farmed, but then we don't live in an ideal world. I reckon those who own large tracts have mostly earned it, and what they do with it is their choice." He shrugged. "It's better than it all being bought up by developers and made into subdivisions."

Seymour nodded grimly. "Rest assured that'll never happen with my land. Not while I'm alive."

"Glad to hear it."

"Why do you still call this the Remingtons' land. You own everything we've ridden on to this point."

That took Chance by surprise. He wondered how Seymour knew that the Remingtons had divided up their land last year, giving an equal portion to their four sons and him. He shrugged. "It doesn't feel like it's mine. The Remingtons passed it on to their sons. They see me as a son, and they gave me an equal share, but I see myself more as a caretaker of their property than the new owner. To me, it'll always be Remington land."

"I thought it must be something like that. Before I met you, I half expected you to tell me that you owned land, that you weren't just a hired hand."

Chance smiled. "But that was before you knew me."

"It was. I'm glad to be wrong—and I don't say that often."

Chance chuckled. "I don't imagine you do. If it's any consolation, I'll admit that I'm glad I was wrong about you, too."

Seymour raised an eyebrow.

"I thought you cared more about what you deem to be right than you did about Hope."

"Well, now you know that's not true."

"I do."

Seymour nodded. "I hope she learns to believe it."

"I think she already has. Whatever happened between the two of you yesterday, it was good. She seems to have a whole new understanding of you."

Seymour smiled. "And I have you to thank for that."

"How?"

"She told me that you remind her a lot of me. That ..." he stopped, seeming uncertain whether he should continue. "That we're alike. That we've both wasted half our lives mourning the women we loved and that she'd like to help us both find happiness again."

Chance pressed his lips together and turned away to stare at the mountains. He didn't want Seymour to see the tears in his eyes.

"Can we cross over there?" Seymour pointed to the irrigation ditch that marked the property line.

Chance nodded. "Sure."

Seymour smiled. "Let's go ride on my land."

Once they'd crossed the ditch, they cantered across the pasture. Chance couldn't help but notice how good the grazing would be here. There'd been no cattle on this land in all the time he'd been in the valley.

"I'm going to suggest something, and I want you to think it over before you answer."

Chance waited, wondering what was coming.

"I own the largest parcel of the best ranch land in the whole valley, and it lies idle. My daughter is talking about moving here to be with you. What would you think of ranching the land for me? I wouldn't interfere, you can run it as you see fit."

Chance shook his head slowly.

"Don't answer. I want you to consider it."

Chance shook his head again, more firmly this time. "I don't need to consider it. I have the Remingtons to think about. I run their cattle; I work their land." He held up a hand when Seymour started to interrupt. "I know it's technically my land now, but to me, it will always be theirs. It's a great offer, and I appreciate where you're coming from. I really do. This isn't about pride or rejecting you or anything like that." He nodded. "It's about loyalty."

"And not wanting to feel owned?"

"No. I don't feel owned by the Remingtons. They're my family. Maybe someday you and I will be family, but my loyalty is to them. They've been so good to me, done so much for me; I couldn't walk away from them now. The cattle ranch isn't the biggest money maker, but it contributes. The guest ranch and the horse stud make more money, but the cattle were Dave's life. I'm keeping his legacy going—if that doesn't sound too dramatic."

Seymour smiled. "It doesn't sound dramatic. It sounds like something I envy."

Chance sighed. "I'd love to help you out, but it wouldn't be right. Maybe you should come back here and ranch it yourself?"

"It's a nice idea, but I couldn't. I'm too good at finding the best person for any job and putting them in place to manage things. I'm not cut out to be a rancher."

"I guess not."

"I hope I didn't offend you? I thought it could be good for all of us."

"I'm flattered, not offended, but I have to stay where I am."

"I understand."

~ ~ ~

Hope paced the back porch of the cabin; she couldn't make herself sit still while she waited for Chance and her dad to get back from their ride. She'd been surprised that they'd gone out together like that. Part of her was thrilled, part of her terrified about what might go on between them while they rode.

She was relieved when she finally saw them come walking up the path from the barn. "I hope you had fun?" she asked before they even reached the porch.

Her dad smiled. "That was the best time I've had in years. You should ride out sometime; you'd love it."

"I know," she said with a laugh. "But he's usually working too hard to have time. You get special consideration because you're you."

Chance chuckled. "You get special consideration, too."

Her dad smiled at them. "I'm going to head back up to the house. Let you two have some time together. I'm sorry I stole him away from you this morning." He turned to smile at Chance. "But I'm glad I did."

"Don't you want to stay for some lunch?" she asked

"No, thanks. I'm going to head back. I hope I'll see you again soon." He pulled his phone out of his pocket and then seemed to change his mind. "I suppose I could walk back to the car all by myself, couldn't I? I don't need to call Ivan to come get me."

Hope smiled. "I think you're safe here, Daddy."

He smiled and tipped his hat to them. "Bye now."

They watched him walk up the path to the parking lot by the guest ranch where Ivan jumped out of the SUV to greet him. Hope turned to Chance. "How did it go?"

"Better than I ever dreamed it might. I like him. I never expected to be able to say that. I thought at best I might learn to understand where he's coming from and maybe convince him that I'm okay." He shook his head. "But I like him; I feel a kinship with him."

Hope grinned. "I'm so glad. I think the two of you have more in common than you know."

His smile faded. "He told me that."

"Oh." She hadn't expected her dad to tell Chance what she'd told him about them both wasting their lives.

Chance nodded. "And you're right, but I think that we both have one more thing in common now. I think we're both ready to move forward in life. Thanks to you."

Hope flung her arms around his neck and kissed him. "I hope so. Is that what the two of you talked about? I've been worrying about you all morning, what he might say to you, what he might ask you. I hope he didn't push you about anything?"

"He didn't. He did ask me something, but I told him no."

"What?"

"We rode out to where the Remington land borders his, and he asked me if I wanted to ranch his land. If I wanted to run a herd for him up there."

"And you said no?" Hope was surprised that her dad had come up with that idea.

"Yeah. I have a job. I run the herd here. This is my place; this is my family."

Hope nodded. She wasn't quite sure what to think of it—of her dad's offer, or Chance's explanation of why he didn't take it. Part of her wanted to say that she wanted to be his family, but she couldn't. "I see."

"Are you disappointed?"

"A little, maybe, I guess." She smiled at him. "I'm sorry. I don't know what to think. I hope you didn't say no because you think it'd be his way to control you?"

"No. That didn't even occur to me." He met her gaze. "If I was worried about anything it was about him maybe controlling you. In some ways, it would be him taking care of you if you came to live here."

She frowned. "When I come to live here."

"Don't you need to figure out what you'd do here before you say when?"

She sighed. "Yes, but I know that I want to. I don't want you to think of it as an if, anymore. I want you to know that I'm going to move here. I talked to Oscar this morning. He said I can have his place as long as I want it."

"Okay."

"What? You're not happy with that?" Her heart sank, she could tell he wasn't.

"The only part I'm not happy with is that you're going to stay at Oscar's." He smiled. "I thought you said you love my cabin?"

"I do, but I wasn't about to invite myself to live with you."

"So, how about if I invite you? Do you think you could stand it? Or would you be better at Oscar's?"

"I'd love it. If you want me?"

"I want you, honey."

He slid his arms around her waist. "I want you to live with me."

"Then as soon as I get back from LA, I'll move in."

"You're going back?"

"Yes. I was going to tell you that next. Toby called this morning. There are a couple of things I need to sort out. I'll only be a few days, and I don't need to go till next week."

Chapter Eighteen

Seymour smiled at his brother and raised his glass to him. "It's good to see you, Johnny."

"It's good to see you, too, especially to see you back here, and smiling."

"It's good to be here. I thought this was going to be a rough visit, but it hasn't been that way at all."

June smiled at him. "Do you like Chance?"

"I do. He's a man I can respect, in many ways."

"You still have doubts, though," said Johnny. "I can tell."

Seymour nodded and took another sip of his bourbon. "Wouldn't you? He seems decent enough now. He has morals; he has a great work ethic, he's honest to a fault. But come on, he beat a man half to death. What father wouldn't have reservations?"

"It was a long time ago," said June. Seymour already knew that she thought the world of Chance. And when it came to Hope, June always took her side. No, that wasn't fair. June tried to step into the role of mother as best she could. She wanted to see Hope happy; that was all.

"It was, and I even understand what drove him to do it, but if a man's got that kind of violence in him, does it ever leave him?"

Johnny shook his head. "I don't think Chance has violence in his nature. I think he had a lot of pain, frustration, and anger about Chloe's death. The violence was an outlet for him. The only outlet he had. And to be fair, he wasn't a man. He was a kid back then; he's become a man since."

Seymour nodded. "I can see all the logic; I want to let go of my doubt." He smiled at June. "I'm not as bad as you think I am. I want her to be happy."

"Oh, Seymour." She reached across and touched his arm. "I know you do. I just think it's been so long since you've allowed yourself any happiness that you don't really know what it is anymore—or what risks most of us will take to find it."

He scowled at her, but she just laughed. "The big bad tough guy act doesn't work on me, remember? I held you while you cried after Kate died. I know the real you, the one who hides behind the harsh exterior."

He nodded. "You're right, but how do I risk Hope's safety?"

Johnny shook his head. "That's not a question you need to answer. It's not your risk to take. A better question would be how do you support her while she takes the risk—she's going to do it anyway. You don't get to make that decision. What you get to decide is what you can do to help her—hopefully to help her be happy. But if it doesn't work out between them, how do you help her get over it? You stick with asking yourself those questions, and you and Hope will both be fine. Your relationship will be stronger, no matter what."

"You're right. I'm so used to making all the decisions; I forget that when it comes to her, they're hers to make. You've just helped me understand something I never have before though. I've stayed away from her because I understand—most of the time—that I shouldn't try to control her. I thought that if I wasn't making her decisions for her, then there was nothing left I could do for her. That I should stay out of the way and let her get on with it."

June sighed and patted his arm again.

"It's okay. I understand now. My role is to support her in whatever she decides." He nodded to himself. "Even if I don't agree, even if I think I can see a better way, I can only offer opinions and guidance. If she doesn't want to take those, I can still give her support. Right?" He looked at them both, feeling rather stupid that he'd never figured that out before.

"Right," said Johnny. "You don't get to orchestrate their life." He smiled. "Believe me. I've wished so many times I could do that with the boys, but it isn't our job as parents. Our job is to support them, to love them through the choices they make—the good and the bad."

Seymour nodded. He understood that now. "I think I screwed up today."

June raised an eyebrow at him. "How?"

"I asked Chance if he wanted to take over my land, run a herd of cattle on it."

"I'd say that was a lovely thing to do," said June with a smile.

Seymour chuckled. "Is that the first time you've ever approved of something I've done?"

She smiled. "Not the first time ever, but the first time in about twenty years."

"I agree," said Johnny. "It was a nice offer. It wasn't a mistake, but I'm sure he didn't accept."

Seymour shook his head. "No. His loyalty is to the Remingtons. Did you know he owns a fifth of that ranch? An equal share with the other brothers?"

Johnny smiled. "No. I didn't, but it doesn't surprise me. Dave and Monique have treated him as one of their own since they took him in."

"He sees them as his own. He turned me down because his loyalty is with them. They're his family."

"You might end up being his family, too," said June.

"I believe I will. I feel there's something inevitable about him and Hope. They remind me of Kate and me in a way."

Johnny nodded. "And why should he have to decide between different sides of his family?"

"What do you mean?"

"I mean, your land adjoins the Remingtons', why not let him run it all as one big ranch. If he and Hope get married, that's no doubt what'll happen when you die."

Seymour nodded slowly. "You might be onto something there."

Johnny nodded. "It could work."

"It wouldn't help Hope, though, would it?" asked June. "It still wouldn't give her any purpose here. What's she going to do?"

Seymour shook his head. "That I don't know. I hear from Bill that she's not engaged with the Athleticwear anymore, but I don't know what she's going to do from here."

"Again," said Johnny, "it's not for you to figure out. That's for her to do."

"I know, I know. I can't help it, though."

June smiled. "I, for one, am proud of you. I never thought you'd be trying to find a way to help her make it happen. I thought you'd be looking for ways to stop her."

"So did I, but she asked me to come with an open mind, and, for once, I did."

Johnny smiled at him. "I'm proud of you as well. And I don't mind telling you that I'm selfishly hoping that things do work out between them."

"Selfishly?"

"Yes. If Hope moves here, if they get married, I think I'll get to see a lot more of you. If they have children, then I know you'll be here more."

June met his gaze. "Maybe you'd even move back in?"

He stared at them. "I've come to terms with a lot since I arrived here yesterday. I'm not going to make any rash decisions."

June smiled at him. "But you'll think about it, won't you?"

"I will." Seymour already was thinking about it. This visit hadn't turned out anything like he'd anticipated. He'd come to rescue his daughter from the clutches of some gold-digger. He'd come back to Paradise Valley because he felt he had to— not through any desire to be here again. What he'd found was a man who loved his daughter, a man who wanted her to be happy; a man who, in some ways, was as broken as he was himself. Yet through that man, and what Hope saw in him, Seymour had seen for the first time since Kate died, that perhaps he could be happy again, and that perhaps keeping his distance—from people and from happiness—wasn't the best way to live the rest of his life.

He got to his feet. "I'm going to sleep at the house tonight."

They both looked shocked. "I thought you were going to stay here?" asked June.

Johnny nodded his understanding. Seymour would need some time to come to terms with the past and with his memories before he'd ever be able to enjoy the present in the valley— and especially in the house. "Do you want me to come up there with you for a nightcap?"

Seymour nodded. He didn't trust himself to speak around the lump in his throat.

~ ~ ~

Hope opened her eyes and stared up at the ceiling. Chance's arm rested across her stomach, and she loved the feel of it. He made her feel safe and protected and loved. Things were going so fast, but so well. Her dad's appearance had made things better between her and Chance. It had helped her understand him better. By comparing him to her dad, she felt she understood them both better. Knowing that her dad liked Chance and wasn't going to stand in their way made her happy. That was one less obstacle they had to overcome. Now, she just had to figure out what she was going to do with herself when she moved here. Chance still had to figure out if he could love her; no, she already knew he did. It wasn't whether he could love her so much as whether he could share his life with her—whether he could accept that the life he'd wanted with Chloe was gone, but that life with her was possible. She believed he'd already made his decision, on a conscious level, but she knew that a decision wasn't enough to combat the feelings when they arose. She wasn't so sure that he wouldn't pull away from her as they started to move forward. He might find that he really couldn't leave Chloe behind, even though she didn't think he had to. There was nothing she could do about that obstacle—nothing except move forward and try.

Of the things she could control, they all seemed to be falling into place. She'd decided she was going to give Cassidy a call this morning. She liked her, and she was hoping that Gina had talked to her and that maybe she could come up with some ideas. Hope didn't mind taking an extended vacation, and she didn't mind; in fact, she quite liked the idea of reinventing herself and starting a new venture. The trouble was she had no idea what she might do. She'd worked as a model even before she finished college. As she'd gotten older, it had seemed natural that she should go on to create her own line of athletic wear. She'd never done anything outside the world of modeling and design. Even though she hadn't been loving it, or feeling engaged with it for the last year or so, if she was honest, she had no clue what else she wanted to do.

Chance's arm tightened around her middle, and he drew her close. "Morning."

She turned and pressed a kiss to his lips. "Morning. Do you want me to make you some coffee?"

"I'll get it, in a minute. There's something else I want more."

She smiled; she knew what was coming. He seemed to always wake up wanting her. "And what's that?"

He smiled and took hold of her hand, drawing it down beneath the sheet to him. He was so hot and hard she smiled. "And what do you want me to do about that?"

He shrugged. "I dunno. I was hoping you might come up with something."

She closed her hand around him and began to stroke up and down the length of him. "Something like this?"

He slid his hand between her legs and stroked her, making her close her eyes. It felt so good.

"I was thinking more about something like this." He circled her clit with his thumb, and she felt herself get wet for him. She rocked her hips in time with his hand while she continued to pump her hand up and down his hot, hard shaft. "Please?" he breathed.

She rolled on top of him, letting her hair dangle down in his face. "Are you going to give me a ride?"

He nodded, and his hands came up to close around her breasts, sending ripples of desire coursing through her. She straddled him and got up on her knees, guiding him toward her entrance. She was in a hurry now; she needed to feel him inside her. His hands came down to grasp her hips, and as he thrust up, she impaled herself on him. She gasped as he filled her and began to move with him. There was nothing slow and gentle about their coupling this morning. He was giving her a ride all right, and all she could do was hang on and go with him. His hips bucked wildly underneath her, and he pulled her down to meet each thrust. She leaned forward to put her hands on either side of his head, and he hit that spot inside her. "Chance!" she gasped.

He smirked and shifted his hands from her hips to her ass, holding her wide open to receive him as he thrust deeper and harder. All she could do was move with him as all the muscles in her belly tightened. He was carrying her away, and she was ready to fly with him.

"I love you, Hope," he cried at the moment he found his release.

"Yes!" she gasped as she went with him, his climax triggering hers, sending wave after wave of pleasure crashing through her. It felt like her orgasm would never end as he pounded into her over and over and she soared away, moaning his name.

When they finally lay still, she turned to kiss his cheek. "I love you, too, Chancey bear."

She could feel his chest rumble underneath her as he chuckled. "Really? You're going to call me that right now, just when I was feeling like a real man—all testosteroned out having shown his woman a good time?"

She laughed. "Yes, you're always my Chancey bear."

He sighed and gently pushed her off him. "If you say so, but you might not want to call me that before we make love."

She gave him a puzzled look, not understanding.

He narrowed his eyes at her and held up a pointed finger. "It makes me go from this, to this." He let his finger droop and curl up.

She laughed and slapped his shoulder. "It doesn't! Does it?"

He nodded solemnly. "If you don't believe me, you can try it sometime, but I promise you we'll both be disappointed."

She laughed. "Okay, note to self, made."

He narrowed his again. "And what did that note say?"

"To only call you Chancey bear at times when there's no hope of you ravishing me anyway."

He laughed. "There's always a chance of that happening."

"That's true. I should make it when it's unlikely that you're going to. Like out in public."

"You wouldn't dare."

She gave him a wicked smile and rolled out of bed. "You know me better than to dare me. I'm going to put the coffee on, or I'll make you late for work."

When he came into the kitchen after his shower, she handed him a mug of coffee.

"Thanks, honey." He dropped a soft kiss on her lips, making her smile, making her want this to be their life.

"What are you doing today?"

"I thought I might go up to town. I want to talk to Cassidy."

He raised an eyebrow. "I thought you'd be going to see your dad."

"I will. He always works for a few hours in the morning. So, I thought I'd go and see Cassidy first and then stop in to see him on the way back down the valley."

Chance nodded. "And when are you going back to LA? I want to take some time off to spend with you before you go."

"I think I'll leave on Monday, so we can get the weekend together before I go. I don't want to mess you up; I know you have to work."

"I do, but I want time with you, too."

"I know, but you took the morning off with my dad yesterday."

He frowned. "You don't mind that I took time with him instead of you, do you?"

She laughed. "Mind? I love that you did that, and it went so well. Though I'll admit that I'm a little jealous that he got to ride out with you and I haven't yet."

"We'll fix that at the weekend. I'll take you out. I'll ask Summer if you can take Lola. She's a sweetheart, and she's not getting out enough while Summer's expecting."

"Thank you. I'd love that."

"Great. Well, I'd better get moving." He poured his coffee into a travel mug and came to give her another kiss. "What have you got going on with Cassidy?"

"I want to pick her brain. Gina says she's the one who has all the great ideas, and I want to see if she can help me figure out what I can do with myself here."

Chance nodded. "She's always full of ideas that one, and they seem to make her a lot of money. I hope she can help."

"Me too."

He stopped when he got to the doorway and looked back at her. "Can I ask you something?"

"What?"

"Does it bother you that I don't have the same kind of money you do?"

"No!"

He nodded. "I'd hate you to feel like you have to work or something."

She smiled and went to him, putting her hand on his arm. "I do feel I have to work, but not for the money. I have to be doing something useful. Like I told you when we were in Oregon, I haven't felt like my work is useful for a while now. I'm looking at this as an opportunity to start something new, hopefully, something that I can value."

He nodded, but he didn't look convinced.

"Chance, I don't know how this sounds, but I'm not used to anyone having the same kind of money I do. It goes with the territory for me. If I didn't want to, I'd never have to work a day in my life. That is a big difference between us, but it doesn't concern me in slightest—as long as it doesn't concern you?"

He shrugged. "I'd be lying if I said it didn't feel a little strange. I guess I'm old school in that respect. I believe a man should be able to provide for his woman."

"And you can. It's not like you don't make any money at all, is it? It seems to me you do quite well for yourself, and you're a landowner, too," she added with a smile trying to lighten things up.

"Yeah. I'm fine with my situation; I just wonder if it's enough for you. If it's going to be enough."

"It is. What matters between us is how we feel, not where the money comes from, right? We have enough to do whatever we want to do, and we always will."

He seemed uncomfortable with that, but he nodded. "I guess."

She smiled. "You can know, you don't have to guess. But for now, you'd better get your butt up to the barn, or you're going to be late."

He smiled and dropped a kiss on her lips. "Okay, you have a good day. I'll see you later. Call me and let me know if you want me to come up to Oscar's after work."

"Thanks, I might. I don't know how long Dad plans to stay."

"Yeah, maybe we should have dinner with him again."

"Maybe, I'll let you know."

Chapter Nineteen

When Chance got to the barn, he was surprised to find Dave Remington sitting on the bench outside drinking his coffee and enjoying the sunshine.

"Morning."

Dave looked up and smiled. "Good morning. You're just the man I was hoping to see."

"Oh yeah? What can I do for you?"

"I don't need you to do a damned thing, son. I just wanted to see you. I haven't seen you in a while. I try to keep out of the way, but retirement doesn't suit me too well. I just want to hear how things are going—with the herd, and with you."

Chance smiled. He knew what this was about. "And with Hope?"

"Yeah." Dave didn't deny it.

"I've wanted to come and talk to you both, but at first I didn't know what I wanted to say because I didn't know what I was doing."

Dave nodded. "I can understand that, and we haven't wanted to stick our noses in. You were so down when you came home after your trip, but now she's here, she's been here for a while, and we haven't heard anything from you."

Chance chuckled. "I bet you've heard enough from the others, though?"

"Monique's been pressing them all for any information she can get. The boys have played dumb, but the girls have been happy to tell anything they know."

Chance smiled. "I should have come to see you both myself."

"It's okay. You don't have to tell us a thing if you don't want to. We just need to know you're okay. I thought I was seeing things when I spotted you and Seymour Davenport riding out together. I hope that went okay? He's not an easy man."

"I don't imagine he is, but he and I hit it off. It seems we have a lot in common."

Dave nodded. "I wondered if you'd both realize that. Kate was a wonderful woman. The whole valley mourned her for a long time. She was taken too young." He met Chance's gaze. "But not as young as your Chloe."

Chance nodded. "Yeah, I think he saw something of himself in me, as crazy as that sounds."

"It doesn't sound crazy to me at all. I can see it. So, do you have his blessing?"

"I do."

"And are the two of you hoping to say I do?"

Chance narrowed his eyes.

Dave smiled. "Sorry, but little Ruby says you are."

He had to smile. "I'd like to think we are, but every time we get past one hurdle, another one crops up."

Dave cocked his head to one side.

"See, I've come to terms with being able to love Hope, with wanting to share my life with her. I never thought I'd be able to say that, but it's true. She's helped me to see that I don't have to leave Chloe behind, that she goes with me everywhere because she's a part of me."

Dave nodded approvingly.

"She's made some peace with her dad, and he's accepted that I'm an okay guy and maybe even worthy of being with his daughter. She's going to move up here and find something to do for a career."

"I'm glad to hear it, but what new hurdle has cropped up now? And how can it be any more major than those you've already overcome?"

Chance shook his head. "It's major in my mind; I need to find a way around it."

"And what is it?"

Chance blew out a sigh. "The money! She's loaded, more than loaded, she's a multi-millionaire in her own right, never mind that when her dad dies, she'll be a billionaire."

Dave nodded. "But you've known that from the start."

"I have, but it's only now that I'm daring to think about us really spending the rest of our lives together that the reality of what that means is starting to sink in. I'm a man, I should provide for her, and I can, but not to the level she's used to. I can give her a home, but the cabin isn't the kind of place she's used to living in."

"So, build something. You've got the land, you can build a nice place, just like Beau has on his land."

Chance sighed. "I know, I could do that, but it still wouldn't be what she's used to."

"It sounds to me like what she's used to isn't what she really wants. She's prepared to give it all up to be with you; she knows what she'd be getting into."

"Yeah, but what if she thinks she should build us a house or buy one? The kind of house that costs millions, like the ones she's always lived in."

Dave shrugged. "What if she does? Would it be a problem?"

Chance shrugged. "It shouldn't be, no. Not if we're a team, but it sure as hell doesn't feel right to me."

Dave nodded. "I'm not making light of it. I do understand. Maybe you should talk to Shane; he's in kind of the same boat with Cassidy. She's made millions. Shane moved into her house which is more like a mansion if you ask me. They do okay. He's no less of a man for it."

Chance nodded. "I know it's stupid, but I have to be honest with myself. I know me, I know I can't be comfortable with it."

"It's wise to know yourself, but maybe you can learn to live with it. She's giving up her life to come here to be with you; maybe you can give up a little of your pride and meet her halfway?"

Chance narrowed his eyes. "It's not about pride! It's about ..." He stopped and thought about it. "Damn! It really is, isn't it?"

Dave nodded. "I hate to break it to you, son, but that's all it is. You need to decide if she's worth more to you than your pride. That's all it comes down to."

"Wow. I guess I've got some thinking to do in the saddle today."

Dave smiled. "I guess you do. You'd better get to it. Can I tell Monique that you're okay, then?"

"Yeah, and tell her I'll bring Hope over to meet her at the weekend? I think they'd both like that."

Dave grinned. "Thank you!"

He stood up and gave Chance a hug. "You're finally getting there, son."

Chance nodded. He hoped so.

~ ~ ~

Hope found a parking spot open right in front of Cassidy's gallery in town. She almost didn't take it; she'd planned to call before she went in, to see if it was okay. She pulled in and peered through the storefront to see if there were any customers in there. Maybe this was a bad idea? She jumped when Cassidy appeared in the window and waved at her enthusiastically, beckoning her to come inside. There was her answer. Apparently, this was a good time.

"Hey!" Cassidy pulled the door open as she reached it. "What a nice surprise. You are here to see me, right? You weren't just parking there to go run errands or something? You looked a bit shocked when you saw me."

Hope smiled. "No, I wanted to come talk to you, but I didn't know if it was too rude to just drop in."

Cassidy laughed. "No way! It's awesome to see you. Come on in; I've just made a fresh pot of coffee. Do you want some?"

"Yes, please."

"Gina told me you're thinking about moving here," said Cassidy as she led her through to the back. "She asked me if I had any bright ideas about what you could do with yourself."

"That's right. I've been drawing a blank."

Cassidy grinned as she picked up the coffee pot and poured them each a mug. "Well, you've come to the right person. I've been giving it some thought, and I have all kinds of ideas. They probably won't suit you, but at least we'll get a better idea of what you want and don't want to do." She handed Hope a mug and gestured for her to take a seat.

Hope looked back toward the door to the gallery. "Don't you need to be out front, in case someone comes in?"

"Nope. I have a buzzer on the front door, and we'll be comfier in here. First, tell me what you enjoy."

Hope shrugged. "I really don't know anymore. I loved modeling at first. It was fun, but after a few years it got old, it's such a bitchy, fickle world, and besides, as I got older it wasn't realistic to think I could keep going forever."

Cassidy nodded. "So, you got into design, started your own line of athletic wear, which I love, by the way. All my workout clothes are Davenport."

Hope smiled, encouraged by Cassidy's enthusiasm. "Thanks."

"But you don't want to keep that up? You don't enjoy it anymore, or you just don't think you can if you live here? You could always travel back and forth if you needed to. It's not like you don't have a private jet, is it?"

Hope shook her head. "I do, but that's not the point. I haven't been very involved at Davenport for a while now. The new designers I brought in are far better than I ever was, and the guys who run the business love what they do in a way that I don't." She shrugged. "It was a natural progression from modeling career wise, but I don't think it was necessarily the right move for me personally."

"Oh, in that case, a lot of my ideas won't make any sense."

"What ideas?"

"Well, I thought you could start a new line, suited to the lifestyle up here. You could do outdoor wear; you know, hiking and camping and fishing and hunting wear. Women are under-served in all those markets. Well, there are a few good lines, but there's room for more, especially if they have your kind of touch. Women still want to look and feel good while they're out in the mountains or on the river. Most of the clothes available are more about utility than style."

Hope nodded, thinking it over. "It's a good idea. It'd make sense to move in that direction ..."

Cassidy shook her head adamantly. "No, it wouldn't. I thought it might, but that was before I knew how you felt about the work you were doing. You don't need to find another logical progression. This is a chance for a whole new start in life. You need to find something you can really enjoy, something you're passionate about—and that will make you decent amounts of money." She smiled. "I know you don't need it, but if you're anything like me, you still feel you have to make it, just because it's a quantifier of success."

Hope smiled. "I am like you. Having the money isn't important, but being able to make it is."

Cassidy nodded. "So, what else do you enjoy?"

Hope shrugged. "Is it sad to admit that I don't really do much? I work, and I work out, but other than that, I go to social events I don't really enjoy and hide out at my house."

Cassidy rolled her eyes. "Girlfriend, you need to make this move. We need to find you a career you can love and get you out and about. There's no fancy social life here, dinners like the one you came to the other night are about as social as it gets, but you can ride, you can hike, you can explore the park. You might find you like painting or photography, or you could try writing."

Hope laughed. "Gina wasn't kidding that you're a fount of ideas."

Cassidy shrugged. "I see possibilities everywhere. Most people can't come up with any ideas; my problem is that I can't narrow them down to the best ones."

Hope shook her head. "I just can't see any, and I'm too good at shooting them down when I do."

"Well, let's cast around. I'm guessing you're creative, given your design skills?"

"I suppose, but I think I'm really more comfortable with the business side of things."

"Wow! Okay. Do you like the people side of the business or the numbers?"

Hope thought about that. "I think I'm better with numbers; they're more predictable and reliable."

Cassidy laughed. "Good to know." Her smile faded. "Your dad's here, isn't he?"

"Yes." Hope wondered what that had to do with anything.

"Well, he's like the biggest numbers guy on earth," Cassidy explained, seeing her puzzled look. "Didn't he start out day trading? And he got so good at it, he set up his own brokerage? And now he runs some of the largest hedge funds on the planet?"

Hope nodded.

"And he's here right now. And you're looking for a way to make a living with a career that doesn't have to be tied to any location. And you like numbers. And forgive me, but from what I hear the two of you are trying to rebuild your relationship."

"Yeah." Hope still didn't get where Cassidy was going.

"So, you ask him to teach you. Not his whole business, you don't want to get into something that's going to take over your life, but you could ask him to teach you day trading. I have plenty of friends back East who live pretty lavish lives from day trading. They love what they do, they're engaged and happy and have as much or as little free time as they want." She grinned. "What do you think?"

Hope nodded slowly. She wasn't sure what to think. Why had it never occurred to her before to follow in her father's footsteps? It had never been a question when she was small. She was a girl. No, that wasn't it. Her mom had died, and from that point on, her dad had withdrawn from her. She'd been determined to make her own way in the world, and, of course, he hadn't approved of her modeling career—which had made her all the more determined to pursue it. She looked up at Cassidy. "It would be a way to spend some time with him, to get him to teach me."

"Yeah! And I'll bet he'd love it. It's obviously important to him, and to be able to share that with you would be pretty awesome for both of you."

Hope smiled. "I could ask him to stay here for a while, to help me find my feet. He'd like that."

Cassidy grinned. "Do you know anything about trading at all?"

Hope shrugged. "A little, I'm not completely ignorant. I've always been kind of interested in the markets."

"There you go then."

Hope smiled. "I think you might be onto something."

Cassidy raised her mug in a toast. "Let's hope so."

Hope headed straight to the house when she left Cassidy. She'd planned to spend some time in town, partly to get to know the place again and partly to give her dad time to be finished with his work before she went to see him. Now, she didn't want to wait. She wanted to talk to him straight away, to see what he'd think of the idea. Maybe he'd think it was stupid, that she wouldn't be suited to it, and, if that was the case, she'd rather find out straight away, before the excitement she was feeling had the time to get hold of her completely.

She stopped in front of Uncle Johnny's. He was kneeling in the shrubs by the front steps and looked up with a smile. "Hi, Hopey. Your dad's up at the house."

"Thanks. I'm going to go straight up there."

"Do you want to wait here a while till he's done with work?"

She shook her head. "No, I really don't." She hoped that for once he might put his work aside for her sake.

She pulled up in the circular driveway and ran up the steps to the grand entrance. Flinging the doors opened she called for him. "Dad? Where are you?"

He appeared at the top of the stairs. "Up here. What's wrong?"

"Nothing's wrong. I just want to talk to you." She grinned and ran up the stairs, greeting him with a hug and a kiss on the cheek.

He beamed. "Whatever's going on, it's worth ending my conference call for. Let me go tell them to carry on without me. I put them on hold."

She followed him into his office and waited while he dismissed the people he'd been talking to. When he turned back to her, he smiled. "I probably shouldn't have done that. It was important. But something about this visit, being here with you, seeing you happy with your Chance, it's making me realize what's truly important, and it isn't that meeting we were in the middle of. So, tell me. What's going on?"

She smiled nervously. Maybe he'd think she was crazy? Maybe he'd think her idea wasn't worth missing his meeting for.

He sat down on the big leather sofa by the window and gestured for her to join him. "Come on; it looks like you're excited about something and I'd like to know what."

"Okay. You know I want to figure out what I can do with myself when I move here?"

He nodded.

"And you know I'm about done with Davenport Athleticwear."

He nodded again. "And now that you are, can I say that I'm glad?"

She raised an eyebrow at him.

"I'm sorry, Hopey, but I always thought you could do so much more than that."

She nodded. "I want to be offended by that, but I agree with you, so I can't." She smiled. "And if I choose to turn it around and look on the bright side, then I'm happy that you never told me how you felt before."

"I know you think I'm an ogre, but I tried to respect what you were doing."

"I don't think you're an ogre and thank you. I hope you're going to like the idea of what I want to do now."

He smiled. "We won't know till you tell me, will we? So, spit it out. What do you want to do?"

"I'd need your help."

He nodded, but she couldn't read his expression. "I don't mean financially; I mean I'd like you to teach me."

"Teach you what?" he asked with an exasperated smile. "What do you want to do that I could teach you anything about?"

"Day trading. I want to learn. I think I'd be good at it, and I like the idea of following in your footsteps."

For a moment, he looked shocked. Hope grew nervous as the silence drew on. Was he about to say no?

He reached over and squeezed her hand. "I love that idea, Hopey. You have no idea how happy that would make me."

She leaned against him and hugged him. "Thank you! I love the idea, just of day trading, but to think that you could teach me, that you might stay here and help me find my feet. That would be the best."

His eyes were shining when he looked down at her. "You want me to stay?"

She nodded. "Please? If you can? I know you could teach me from anywhere, but I'd love it if you were right here, if I could see you every day, if we could work together."

He nodded. "I'd love that, too."

Hope sat up and looked around at his office and out onto the landing leading to the grand staircase. It was all so familiar; this house had been her only home. Her eyes filled with tears, but she smiled.

"What is it?" asked her dad.

She squeezed his hand. "I think this really is a new beginning. We're back here, in this house, and we're both smiling and excited about the future."

His eyes filled with tears, but he, too, smiled through them and nodded. "I think it's about time."

Chapter Twenty

Chance didn't normally take the whole weekend off, but he'd organized the guys to cover everything so that he shouldn't be needed until Monday. He'd taken Hope out riding this morning, and they'd had a great time. He was thinking about buying her a horse of her own. That was something he could do for her. He'd given a lot of thought to his conversation with Dave the other morning. It was true that his only problem with the financial differences between him and Hope was his pride. Knowing that made it a little easier to accept, but it still bothered him.

"What are you thinking?" she asked.

He smiled. "I'm thinking I'm a lucky son of a gun to have found you."

"I think I'm the lucky one." She checked her watch. "What time do you think we need to get ready?"

"Not for ages yet." They were going over to the cottage to have dinner with Dave and Monique this evening, but right now they were sitting out on the porch, enjoying the late afternoon sun. "Are you nervous?"

"Yes, of course, I am. They're your parents." She frowned. "But they're not really, are they? You've still got your dad and Alice. I loved them when I met them in Oregon."

Chance nodded. "I'm lucky. I get two sets of parents."

"You're very lucky indeed." Hope stared out into the distance. Chance had a feeling she was thinking about her mom, but he didn't want to bring it up in case she wasn't. "Will you take me to see them sometime soon?"

He chuckled. "I'm going to have to. Otherwise Missy will be coming up demanding to meet you."

"I can't wait to meet her. She sounds wonderful."

"She is, I think the two of you will get along well, and I'll have to watch myself."

She laughed. "When can we go?"

"I don't know, when do you think you'll be back from LA?"

Her smile faded. "I shouldn't be too long. I'll need a couple of days to sort things out at the office. They have everything covered, but the way things are right now, they still need my input on some things. I want to set it up so that I'm not part of the system at all. I'll still have to go back sometimes, but not too often."

"Maybe we can go to Summer Lake for a long weekend after you get back."

"I hope so. I can't wait."

Chance nodded. In a way, he was looking forward to taking her. He knew his dad and Alice wanted to see her again, and Missy was starting to get impatient with him now. Part of him wasn't so sure. He didn't know how he felt about taking her there. Summer Lake was Chloe's home. He sighed. Chloe's home was in his heart.

"You don't have to take me if you don't want to." Hope seemed to have read his mind again.

"I do want to, but it's going to be weird the first time."

"I know, just like being back in the house here with Dad is weird for me. It gets easier, though."

"You're going to lay down a whole bunch of new memories there over the next couple of months. Hopefully good memories of the two of you working together."

"We are. I'm excited to get started. Dad's going to stay here while I go back to LA. He said he's going to send things up so that he can be here most of the time now. I never thought I'd see the day he'd call this place home again."

Chance smiled. "It seems as though all three of us are coming to terms with the past and setting up future."

"We are, and I love that my future is with you, here."

"I do too. I love you, honey."

"And I love you, my Chancey bear."

He narrowed his eyes at her, but she shrugged. "You may as well get used to it; I'm not going to stop calling you that."

"I know, but I can hope."

She laughed. "You can hope all you like, but you'd still better get used it."

"I'm getting used to having Hope in my life."

"And I'm getting used to having a Chance."

He smiled. "How corny are we?"

"Totally, but it's hard to not play on our names, isn't it?"

"It is. I feel hopeful about our chance at a future."

She met his gaze. "I do, too. We're working our way past everything that stands in the way, though I still see one big issue that we haven't talked about yet."

"What's that?" Chance hadn't mentioned his feelings about money to her yet; he was hoping he could get some perspective on it himself first. Maybe she felt it, too?

She sighed. "It hasn't mattered while we've been up here, but I think that might change once I move here, especially since Dad's going to be here, too."

"What are you talking about?" It didn't sound like she was referring to the fact that she was rich and he wasn't.

"Sorry, I thought it had been on your mind too. I mean the press."

"Oh." Chance had conveniently forgotten about the public scrutiny that was such a big part of her life. "Do you think they'll follow you up here?"

She shrugged. "I don't know. They tend to show up everywhere I go, but this is so out of the way, maybe they won't. At least not until something newsworthy happens."

"Like you getting a new boyfriend?"

She nodded. "Or like Seymour Davenport moving back into the house he left twenty years ago. The press loves it when something about mom comes up. Dad's noticeable lack of female company since she died has always intrigued them. For a long time, they wanted to paint him as the world's most eligible widower. Now I think they're convinced he has a companion but keeps her hidden. They'd love to uncover his secret, but he really doesn't have one."

Chance shook his head. "I don't understand the whole media thing. I don't understand why anyone would want to intrude on others' privacy and write stories about them for a living, and I don't understand why people would ever want to read those stories. Don't they have enough going on in their own lives? Why do they care about yours?"

"I don't know; I don't get it myself. It's just one of those things that have always been that way. I grew up with it. I'm used to it." She met his gaze. "But you're not, and I know you don't like it."

"I don't, but I accept that it's one of the costs of being with you."

She smiled.

"Can I remind you of that next time you see a camera pointed at us and you want to smash the guy?"

He sighed. "You can. I'll just need to learn to control my temper."

"That'd be nice."

"I'll try." He knew he'd have to deal with the press if he was going to have a future with her, and he was certain now that he was.

His phone rang, and he fished it out of his back pocket, hoping there wasn't a problem with the herd that he'd have to go deal with. It was Monique.

"Hi," he answered.

"Hello, darling. We can't wait to see you both."

He smiled. She was probably checking that he wasn't going to back out. "We're looking forward to it, too. Don't worry; we'll be over at six-thirty."

She laughed. "Good, but I wasn't calling to check on you. I have a question for you both."

"Oh, yeah, what's that?"

"We ran into Seymour today, and we'd like to invite him to join us. Would that be all right with you and with Hope?"

"Hang on." He covered the mouthpiece carefully with his hand and looked at Hope. "It's Monique. How would you feel if your dad joined us?"

"They invited him?" She looked surprised.

"Apparently."

She nodded, looking puzzled. "It's fine by me; it'd be nice to see him."

"Okay." He brought the phone back up to his ear. "It's fine by us if that's what you want."

"It is." He could hear the smile in her voice.

"I didn't know you guys were that friendly with him."

She laughed. "We've known him for years, though we don't normally socialize. It seems we'll have reason to get to know each other better in the future and this seemed a good opportunity to get reacquainted. Plus, we may have an idea we want to run by you."

"Okay. We'll see the three of you in a little while."

"Bye, darling."

He shook his head as he hung up wondering what she and Dave might be cooking up with Seymour.

"Does it seem odd to you?" asked Hope.

"Very. She said the three of them might have an idea they want to run by us."

Hope frowned. "Did it sound like something good?"

He laughed. "I have no idea. I guess we'll just have to wait and see."

"I guess so. I should probably start getting ready. Do you mind if I take the first shower?"

"No, you go ahead. I think I'm going to give my dad a quick call. I feel like I'm leaving him out. I know it's dumb, but we're having dinner with your dad and my other parents. I want to feel like I'm including him, too."

She smiled. "So sweet."

He narrowed his eyes at her. "Weren't you going for a shower?"

"No, not yet. Please, can I say hello to him before I go?"

"Yeah," Chance smiled. He liked the idea that she didn't want to leave his dad out either.

He dialed the number and waited. "Hello?"

"Hey, Alice."

"Chance! We were just talking about you."

"You were? Nothing terrible I hope."

She laughed. "No, we were wondering how you and Hope were doing."

"And wondering when you're going to bring her to see us!" his dad shouted in the background.

"Tell him soon. I'll bring her down there in a couple of weeks, okay. She's right here though, if you want to talk to her."

"Why don't you put her on speaker, and I'll do the same with your dad? I won't be able to hear a thing for him shouting otherwise."

"Okay." He turned to Hope. "I'm putting you on speaker with both of them."

"Hello?" his dad's voice blared out.

"Hi Frank, hi Alice. How are you both?" asked Hope.

"I'm doing a whole lot better since I visited your uncle. He's a miracle worker, but I'm not as good as I will be when you come to see us."

Hope laughed. "We're working on it. I have to go back to LA next week, but when I get back, we're going to make time to come see you."

"Good, don't take too long about it, will you?"

"Frank! They've both got busy lives, we have to be patient," said Alice.

"I don't do patience."

Hope laughed. "So that's where Chance gets it from?"

Chance loved the sound of his dad's laughter. "Yeah, probably, and I guess you've got me to blame that he's such an ornery son of a gun, too."

Hope laughed. "No, you're both sweetie pies."

Chance rolled his eyes at her and Alice laughed loudly. "Either you don't know them too well yet, or you've already figured out how to handle them."

"I think I'm getting the hang of it, but I'm hoping you'll give me some pointers when I see you?"

"I'll try, but most of the time I just hang on and go along for the ride."

Hope waggled her eyebrows at Chance. "Me too."

Chance tried not to laugh. He doubted Alice meant the same kind of ride Hope did.

"What are you kids up to this evening?" asked his dad. "It's Saturday night. Why are you home calling us? Shouldn't you be out partying?"

"We're on our way out, but I hadn't called you for a few days, and I wanted to check in."

"Oh." His dad sounded disappointed.

"What's up?"

"Nothing. I just thought maybe you had some news for us, that maybe you were calling to make an announcement."

Hope smiled, and Chance had to smile with her. It was a good thing they were already talking about the possibility of getting married; this could be an awkward moment if they weren't.

"Like Alice said, you need to be patient."

"I have been. I've been waiting ever since Oregon."

Hope laughed.

"Don't worry. I don't plan to keep you waiting too much longer."

Hope's eyes widened, and he heard Alice gasp. He grinned and shrugged at Hope. "We all know it's coming; I don't see the point in wasting much time."

"Oh, Chance, that's wonderful!" said Alice.

"Just hurry up about it, would you?" asked his dad.

Hope just smiled at him; that must be the happiest he'd seen her yet. He hadn't given much thought to the timing of things before, but now he'd said it, he wanted them to just get on with it. If they were going to get married, what was the point in waiting? "I'll keep you posted, but we'd better get going. I'll call you again soon."

"Take care, son. You be careful in LA, Hope, get back to the mountains as soon as you can. It's safer up there."

"I will, and when I get back, we'll figure out when we can come and see you."

"I'll look forward to it."

"Me too," added Alice. "Love to you both."

"See you guys," said Chance. "Love you."

When he hung up, Hope came around the table to sit on his lap. "So, you don't plan on waiting too much longer?"

He slid his arms around her waist and hugged her to him. "I don't. Do you?"

"I don't want to, no, but I will if you need more time."

"For what?"

She shrugged. "To be sure."

"I am sure. We're going to hit bumps in the road; there are still details that are going to come and bite us in the ass, no question about it, but isn't that the same for everyone? We want to be together; nothing's going to get in the way of that now. So, I'd rather we made it official and face whatever life throws at us as a couple."

She nodded. "Me too."

~ ~ ~

When they were ready, they decided to walk over to the cottage. Hope had seen the place before, but she'd never been down there. It sat behind the barn a little ways, on the other side of the creek. Chance had told her that Mason and Gina used to live there, but now that Dave had officially retired and let the guys take over running the ranch, he and Monique had moved down here while Mason and Gina had taken over the main house.

Chance took hold of her hand as they walked by the barn and she smiled up at him.

"Don't say it," he said out of the corner of his mouth.

She laughed. "What that you're sweet? I wasn't going to, but now that you mention it…"

He shook his head at her. "I think you'll love Dave and Monique."

"I'm sure I will, I just hope they'll like me."

"They're going to love you."

"I think I remember her. She's French, isn't she?"

"Yeah, maybe she'll be able to help you since you're kind of the same."

"How do you mean?"

"She was some society lady in Paris before she met Dave. She came out here to visit Yellowstone, met a cowboy in a bar and never went home."

"Really?"

Chance nodded. "That's the story anyway."

Hope smiled. "I'll have to ask her about it, but I like the idea of us turning out like them. They seem to have had a long and happy life together, they've raised all you boys, and now they're retired and enjoying life."

Chance nodded, looking thoughtful. "If we can turn out like them, I'll be happy."

Hope would, too.

As they got closer to the cottage, they could hear voices out at the back and Chance led her around to the patio. It was beautiful, like a storybook cottage with lovely flower beds.

"There you are," said Dave when he spotted them. "Come on in."

Chance opened the gate and let Hope go ahead of him. Her dad got up from his seat and came to greet them with a smile. "I hope you don't mind me joining you?"

"Of course not, it's a lovely surprise," said Hope as she kissed his cheek.

He turned to shake Chance's hand. "You're going to have to get used to seeing me around, so this is good practice."

Chance nodded. "I'm glad you came."

Monique came out from the house and beamed at them. "Hope! It's so lovely to see you." She came straight to her and wrapped her in a warm hug, before kissing both her cheeks. Hope loved her instantly; there was something so warm and welcoming about her. She felt like a mother figure, and Hope desperately needed one of those—not that she'd known it until that moment.

"Let her go," said Dave with a smile. "I want to say hello, too." He edged his wife away and gave her a warm hug of his own. He felt so strong, and she could see where the Remington boys got their looks from. He was still a good-looking man.

"It's lovely to meet you."

Her dad smiled. "Though you don't know you're not meeting them for the first time."

She looked at Monique. "Were you friends with my mom?"

Monique nodded. "She was a wonderful woman. I still miss her."

Hope looked at her dad. They didn't normally talk about her mom much at all; she hoped she wasn't upsetting him.

He smiled at Dave, then at her. "Your mom and Monique helped each other adapt to living out here." He nodded at Monique. "They both had a lot of adapting to do."

Monique smiled. "We did, but it was well worth it. Your mom loved it here."

Hope couldn't help it; she went to Monique and hugged her again. She wanted to feel close to this woman who'd been her mother's friend.

Monique smiled and patted her shoulder. "Do you want to come help me?"

Hope nodded, glad to get a moment alone with her. She didn't know what she wanted to say, just that she wanted to be around her. Monique felt like a link to her mom.

She looked back and smiled at Chance as she followed Monique inside. He winked at her and nodded before turning to take the beer Dave offered him.

Chapter Twenty-One

Chance was enjoying this evening. He smiled over at Hope who was sitting beside Monique, chatting happily with her. It seemed he'd been right that the two of them might connect. He was glad to see it.

Monique had made them a wonderful meal, and while they'd eaten Dave and Seymour had entertained them with stories of how life used to be in the valley. Chance had been surprised how well they got along. They acted like old buddies, but Dave had never mentioned knowing the Davenports before. Now they were sitting on the patio, Dave had lit the fire pit, and they were enjoying after-dinner drinks. Chance was a little on edge because there'd been no mention of any idea to run by them during dinner. They must be saving it for later—and later must be coming any minute now.

Dave smiled at Hope. "I understand that when you come back from LA, you're going to be staying here full-time?"

"I am." She looked at Chance, and he nodded, knowing she was wondering how much she should say. As far as he was concerned it was up to her how much they told people about their plans. She turned to Seymour. "Dad's going to be teaching me about trading, and ..." She gave her dad a meaningful look. "I'm going to move into the cabin with Chance."

Chance sucked in a deep breath, wondering what Seymour's reaction might be.

He nodded slowly but didn't say anything immediately.

Monique smiled at Chance. "You'll have to start thinking about a bigger place."

Chance nodded. He'd think about any place Hope wanted, but right now he was more concerned what her dad thought.

Seymour met his gaze. "I think that brings us neatly to the idea we want to discuss with you."

Chance nodded and waited; he had no clue what was coming.

Dave grinned at him. "Sorry, son, but we got talking." He smiled at Seymour. "We think we've hit on something that might benefit all of us."

Chance nodded again.

"When we rode out, and you refused my request to run a herd of cattle on my land, I was surprised—pleasantly so—by your refusal. Your loyalty to Dave is admirable."

Chance nodded. He didn't think it was admirable, but it was non-negotiable. If Seymour was about to repeat the offer, he wasn't going to take it, even if Dave said he should. He'd said no, and he meant it. He didn't need Seymour thinking he could come in and talk Dave around to what he wanted.

Seymour smiled. "Would you relax? Dave and I want to run something else by you. I haven't come here to get Dave on my side to make you do what I want."

Chance did relax a little, glad that Seymour could see how this must look to him. "Okay, but tell me already."

Seymour laughed. He no doubt wasn't used to being told to hurry up, but Chance wasn't about to start bowing and scraping to him.

"Okay. I want you to run cattle on my land. Dave wants you to run cattle on his land. Our properties share a border, which could be opened up so that one large herd would have access to both. What do you say? Do you want to expand your operation?"

Chance looked at Dave; he needed to know what he thought first.

Dave grinned encouragingly. "I think it's a fantastic idea. Everybody wins. If you want to do it."

Seymour smirked at him. "I've done my homework. What I have in mind would have you managing the largest herd in the valley. If you'd be up to that. It'd be a big job."

Chance smiled through pursed lips. He knew damned well what Seymour was doing. He was taunting him, poking his ego to say of course he could do it, of course, he was up to the job—and it was working. He nodded. "I could handle it all right, but what's in it for you?"

Hope, Monique and Dave all looked a little taken aback by the direct question, but it was one that needed to be asked.

"You know what's in it for me. You're going to be an important part of my daughter's life." He smiled. "You're going to be an important part of my life. I'd like to see you happy and fulfilled. I'd like to know that you're commanding a salary worthy of the biggest rancher in Paradise Valley. And I'd like to think that since your parcel of Remington Ranch is the closest to my house, you might build your own place on that end, so I'll be closer to you both." He chuckled. "And so that my daughter won't be living in a tiny cabin for too long."

Chance had to laugh with him. "Yeah, I was concerned about that, too."

"I wasn't!" said Hope.

Monique smiled at her. "With the best intentions in the world, you'll still want out of that cabin before the year is out, dear. Believe me."

Dave laughed. "If our experience is anything to go by, I'd start building now, if I were you, Chance!"

He looked around at them all. They were all so happy, they saw this as possible and workable, and the strangest part was that he did, too. He turned back to Seymour. "We'd have to write up a contract."

Seymour laughed. "I have my lawyers drafting one, and, of course, I'll expect it to go through several revisions and negotiations before we agree to terms."

Chance smiled. "Then, in principle, I guess it's a yes."

Seymour got to his feet, and Chance joined him to shake his hand. "Thank you. This means more to me than you know."

Chance nodded. He felt as though he had some idea. Seymour had no interest in cattle. If he did, he would have done something about it at some point in the last twenty years. This was about securing his daughter's future. He looked over at Hope, who looked a little concerned. He knew she was worried her dad was trying to control them somehow, but Chance didn't see it that way. Seymour's intentions were good. He knew it.

~ ~ ~

When they were back at the cabin, Hope led Chance out onto the back porch. She'd had a great time, right up until the point where her dad had made Chance that offer. Since then, she'd been in turmoil. She wanted to believe that her dad was looking out for her and for Chance, but she had a niggling doubt that he was going back to his old ways—trying to direct her life.

"You're worried about what your dad's up to you aren't you?"

"I am. Aren't you?"

"No. I'm not. He's trying to help you, not control you."

"What about you? Don't you feel that by getting you to work for him, he's trying to control you?"

"No. I don't. I think he's trying to help us get a good start on our life together. He already understands who I am and how I work. I won't sign anything that has sneaky clauses in it, and I know an excellent lawyer, Gabe. You'll meet him when we go to Summer Lake. I don't think your dad's trying to string me up though, honey. I don't. I think you need to relax."

"I hope you're right."

"I think I am."

"Okay, then, I'll relax about it. If I believe that it's for the right reasons, then it's an awesome thing for him to do, isn't it?"

Chance smiled. "It is. I love the idea. Like he said, we all win. That doesn't happen too often in life."

"No, it doesn't. I'm going to put my doubts aside and be happy about it."

"I think you should."

He came to her and wrapped his arms around her. "It seems to me we've got a lot to be happy about these days. We've got a new life ahead of us, and it's all just about to begin."

She nodded against his chest, feeling happier than she ever had, standing here with this wonderful man underneath the big starry Montana sky.

"I love you, Chance."

"I love you, Hope. I can't wait to see where we go from here."

Hope smiled as she hugged him tightly. They'd come so far, overcome so much already. She knew it wouldn't be clear sailing from here on, but she believed that the biggest of their problems were behind them;

A Note from SJ

I hope you're enjoying the journey with Chance and Hope. You won't have too long to wait to see what happens next.

Book Three is called Give Hope a Chance and will release on July 11.
If you haven't already visited, Chance has his own page on my website.

www.SJMcCoy.com

If you haven't read my other books, be sure to check out the Remington Ranch series, where you'll see Chance with his adopted family. You can get started with book one, Mason, which you can download in ebook form for FREE from all the major online retailers.
If you haven't read the Summer Lake series yet, you can start that for free too. The boxed set of the first three books is available for download from the major online retailers.

If you'd like to keep in touch, there are a few options to keep up with me and my imaginary friends:

The best way is to Join up on the website for my Newsletter. Don't worry I won't bombard you! I'll let you know about upcoming releases, share a sneak peek or two and keep you in the loop for a couple of fun giveaways I have coming up :0)
You can join my readers group to chat about the books on Facebook or just browse and like my Facebook Page.

I occasionally attempt to say something in 140 characters or less(!) on Twitter

And I'm always in the process of updating my website at www.SJMcCoy.com with new book updates and even some videos. Plus, you'll find the latest news on new releases and giveaways in my blog.

I love to hear from readers, so feel free to email me at AuthorSJMcCoy@gmail.com.. I'm better at that! :0)

I hope our paths will cross again soon. Until then, take care, and thanks for your support—you are the reason I write!
Love
SJ

PS Project Semicolon

You may have noticed that the final sentence of the story closed with a semi-colon. It isn't a typo. Project Semi Colon is a non-profit movement dedicated to presenting hope and love to those who are struggling with depression, suicide, addiction and self-injury. Project Semicolon exists to encourage, love and inspire. It's a movement I support with all my heart.

"A semicolon represents a sentence the author could have ended, but chose not to. The sentence is your life and the author is you."

- Project Semicolon

This author started writing after her son was killed in a car crash. At the time I wanted my own story to be over, instead I chose to honour a promise to my son to write my 'silly stories' someday. I chose to escape into my fictional world. I know for many who struggle with depression, suicide can appear to be the only escape. The semicolon has become a symbol of support, and hopefully a reminder – Your story isn't over yet

Also by SJ McCoy

Summer Lake Series
Love Like You've Never Been Hurt (FREE in ebook form)
Work Like You Don't Need the Money
Dance Like Nobody's Watching
Fly Like You've Never Been Grounded
Laugh Like You've Never Cried
Sing Like Nobody's Listening
Smile Like You Mean It
The Wedding Dance
Chasing Tomorrow
Dream Like Nothing's Impossible
Ride Like You've Never Fallen
Live Like There's No Tomorrow

Coming Next
We will be visiting the lake again, I promise. There are still a couple of weddings I'd like to invite you to AND there is a whole bunch of new characters who have been not-so-patiently waiting for their own stories.

Remington Ranch Series
Mason (FREE in ebook form)
Shane
Carter
Beau
Four Weddings and a Vendetta

A Chance and a Hope

About the Author

I'm SJ, a coffee addict, lover of chocolate and drinker of good red wines. I'm a lost soul and a hopeless romantic. Reading and writing are necessary parts of who I am. Though perhaps not as necessary as coffee! I can drink coffee without writing, but I can't write without coffee.

I grew up loving romance novels, my first boyfriends were book boyfriends, but life intervened, as it tends to do, and I wandered down the paths of non-fiction for many years. My life changed completely a few years ago and I returned to Romance to find my escape.

I write 'Sweet n Steamy' stories because to me there is enough angst and darkness in real life. My favorite romances are happy escapes with a focus on fun, friendships and happily-ever-afters, just like the ones I write.

These days I live in beautiful Montana, the last best place. If I'm not reading or writing, you'll find me just down the road in the park - Yellowstone. I have deer, eagles and the occasional bear for company, and I like it that way :0)

Made in the USA
Middletown, DE
02 April 2019